KILLARNEY

KILLARNEY

KEVIN CALLAN

Stoddart

A BOSTON MILLS PRESS BOOK

This book is dedicated to the people of Killarney,
for the rugged mountains of La Cloche may represent the heart of the land,
but the warm character of its people symbolizes its soul.

Canadian Cataloguing in Publication Data

Callan, Kevin
    Killarney
    ISBN 1-55046-108-8

1. Killarney Provincial Park (Ont.) – Guide-books.
2. Killarney Provincial Park (Ont.) – History.
3. Hiking – Ontario – Killarney Provincial Park – Guide books.
4. Canoes and canoeing – Ontario – Killarney Provincial Park – Guide-books.
I. Title.

Published by
Stoddart Publishing Co. Limited
34 Lesmill Road
Toronto, Canada
M3B 2T6
(416) 445-3333

Design by John Denison/Lexigraf
Typography by Lexigraf, Tottenham
Printed in Canada

A BOSTON MILLS PRESS BOOK
The Boston Mills Press
132 Main St.
Erin, Ontario
N0B 1T0

American Association
for State and Local History
Award of Merit

Winners of the
Heritage Canada
Communications Award

Second Printing: June 1994

The publisher gratefully acknowledges the support of the Canada Council, Ontario Ministry of Culture and Communications, Ontario Arts Council and Ontario Publishing Centre in the development of writing and publishing in Canada.

Contents

Author and his faithful travelling companion, Frodo the ferret, who accompanied him through the interior of Killarney Provincial Park. – David Marcovitz

Acknowledgements

I wish to acknowledge the following people not only for their assistance, guidance and the valuable information they provided during the development of this book, but also for their true friendship.

Special thanks goes to Superintendent John McBreth and the staff of Killarney Provincial Park, as well as to Norm Richards of the Ministry of Natural Resources, Provincial Parks Department.

I would also like to thank Hikers Haven, in Oakville and Unionville, for the use of the 15-foot Kevlar canoe, which they so graciously lent me for the duration of my project. The lightweight canoe was a tremendous asset for paddling and portaging throughout the interior of Killarney Provincial Park and on Georgian Bay.

And last, but certainly not least, I would like to thank the people of Killarney, especially Elizabeth Barron (former resident of Collins Inlet), Billy Burke, Tall Tale Willy, Trapper Darcy, and Teddy de la Morandiere and family. By the way, Ted, how's the dock holding up?

Kevin Callan
Peterborough, 1990

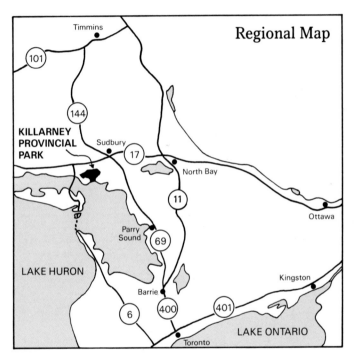

See pages 60-61 for park map.

Killarney Lake from Blue Ridge.

"Nature bestowed all these gifts with a smile
the emerald, the shamrock, the blarney;
when you can purchase all these wonderful things
then you can buy Killarney."

Old Irish folk song

Introduction

As a boy I would head out every Saturday morning to the forested escarpment just a short bicycle ride north of my home town. When I reached the familiar unmarked trail leading to a small brook hidden within a cedar glen, I would quickly hide my bicycle in some brush and sprint down the path toward my private paradise, a little bit of heaven which happened to contain dozens of speckled trout.

After my Saturday-morning adventures I always looked forward to Monday at school, when groups of avid anglers would gather around to listen to my tales of the secret spot. There was one problem, however. I seemed to suffer from something that all true fishermen are cursed with, the gift of the gab. As a result, my fishing competitor and arch enemy, Tommy Baker, finally figured out the location of my fishing hole.

The next weekend, as usual, I headed for my small brook to try my luck. To my horror, I discovered that Tom had beat me to it and had already caught twice his limit. As if that wasn't bad enough, at school on Monday the little marauder had the nerve to spin a better tale than I ever had.

Tom's invasion was just the beginning. Slowly more fishermen discovered the trout-filled stream. The insignificant trail leading to my favourite fishing hole soon became a highway for dozens of designer anglers clad in their top-of-the-line sportswear. My private paradise was eventually dredged out and developed into a stocked trout pond. Next came a picnic shelter, two acres of cut grass, a parking lot for over a hundred vehicles, and even a washroom facility, on the very same spot where I once built a small fire to fry my catch. I have yet to forgive Tommy Baker for helping to destroy my secret spot.

When I think back to that dreadful experience, another paradise always comes to mind: Killarney. It seems like every time I visit this area I see a little more evidence of young Tom's presence on the lakes where I once canoed without spotting a soul. It appears that the secret's out for Killarney. Parts of this once rugged, secluded land have been transformed into a "hotel wilderness."

I guess instead of complaining about the intrusion, my lack of privacy, or the loss of a true wilderness experience, I could venture off and explore other unique areas of Ontario, such as the nearly endless chain of lakes in Algonquin or the pine forests of Temagami, but the last time I visited Algonquin and Temagami, Tom had already been there before me. No, I think I'll stand my ground this time and learn from the past. Instead of praying that characters like Tom don't find and eventually invade my new secret spot called Killarney, I have decided to invite him, and you, along with me. I want to show everyone just how precious Ontario's crown jewel really is, and most of all, how to care for it before it comes to resemble my secret fishing hole back home.

As Old As The Hills

About three and a half billion years ago, scalding steam and poisonous gases burst from open wounds in the earth, quake activity constantly shifted layers of sediment, and finally rock pierced the rolling waves of the gigantic ocean that covered what is now called Northern Ontario. This land formation, an island called "The Superior Province," underwent dramatic changes during the next several hundred million years. Large chunks of its southern shore were eroded, creating "The Southern Province." In the Killarney region, sediment exceeded seven miles in depth, and these layers, caught between rising land and the weight of the ocean, formed different varieties of rock, which eventually buckled, thrust upward and became what we now call the La Cloche Mountain Range, one of the oldest mountain ranges in the world. Approximately 75 percent of Killarney Provincial Park is made up of this ancient quartzite.

Approximately two billion years ago another mountain formation occurred. These granite peaks, generally pink to red in colour, make up roughly 15 percent of the park.

Less than two billion years ago the La Cloche Range towered as high as the Rockies. The main range to the north extends west about 30 kilometres. The two lesser ranges, Blue Ridge and Killarney Ridge, rise up from Georgian Bay to merge with Silver Peak, the point of highest elevation.

One million years ago, the ice age, advancing and retreating four times over, scoured the quartzite peaks, stripping them of soil, grinding and scarring their surfaces, and leaving behind sand, gravel and boulders. As the ice melted, a huge lake was formed, with a water level well above that of present-day Lake Huron. The La Cloche Range was thus transformed into a cluster of white-capped islands.

Today the young Rockies of the West boast higher elevations than the La Cloche, as do the sister peaks of the Laurentians. But if the hills of Killarney could talk, they would spin a historic tale far more grand and ancient than anything the Rockies could possibly muster up.

Killarney's geological boundary: The pink rock along the northern shore of Little Sheguiandah Lake is granite, while the white ridges towering behind are the quartzite hills of the La Cloche Mountain Range.

Land Of Nomads And Mastodons

Excluding the theories that 30,000 years ago, before the last glaciation, prehistoric man excavated the quartzite of Killarney's white-capped mountains, and that nomadic Paleo-Indians came to La Cloche during their extended hunting expeditions, it is generally believed that natives called the Plano people were the first to establish themselves in the area, becoming North America's original settlers approximately 10,000 years ago.

The Plano lived a semi-nomadic existence, venturing out from the quartzite mountains or island peaks (the water level quite high at the time). Based on the discovery of a large quartzite spearhead in the valley of a small river in Grey County, Ontario, archaeologists have speculated about possible routes taken by the Plano or late Paleo-Indian hunters from Killarney, where the spearhead originated. Two possible routes could have been used by the nomadic hunters, either around Georgian Bay or directly across a land bridge that may have connected Manitoulin Island to the Bruce Peninsula when post-glaciation water levels were at least 33 metres below the level of present-day Lake Huron.

This early culture, armed with crude quartzite projectiles, stalked mastodons and caribou along the edge of the retreating glacier and hunted gigantic elk in the mist-filled valleys of spruce and fir.

Archaeologist Emerson Greeman worked in Killarney during the 1930s and discovered a number of Plano sites, including those at George Lake, Chikanishing Creek and Killarney Bay.

The George Lake site predated previous records of man's existence in the area. A hundred metres above the present level of Lake Huron, Greeman uncovered an ancient beach which was occupied by natives roughly 9,000 years ago. Here the Plano people chipped the surface of the white rock for tools and weapons, leaving behind 40,000 quartzite flakes, 400 shattered artifacts, and countless broken quartzite spearheads, knives, and chopping tools.

The Chikanishing Creek site was established some 6,500 years ago, when water levels were 16 to 22 metres above present-day Lake Huron. Water levels rose and fell once more before the Woodland Indians made permanent camp, with the last occupation of the site around 1800 B.C.

Greeman noted that two cultural levels had used the beach sites on Killarney Bay. Adena–Middlesex being the lower level and Point Peninsula the upper level. The 9-metre beach held potsherds and quartzite flakes dating back to 1500 B.C. After that date the native culture expanded and the area became home to the Hopewell people. An Indian chieftain's grave site revealed some of the possessions valued by this culture. The Manitoulin *Expositor* reported Greeman's discovery in 1952: "Unique among the articles recovered were three beautifully fashioned flint ceremonial spear points, six inches long, to which were still attached part of the original wooden shafts. The human bones found appeared to have been wrapped in a beaver-skin bag closed with a copper spindle seven inches long. The matted beaver hair and bones formed a deposit more than two inches thick which was preserved by the action of copper celts or axes and hundreds of copper beads found with it . . . Sixteen large shell spherical beads also found with his remains were made from [conch shell], nearest occurrences of which are the Gulf of Mexico . . . ."

Following the Hopewell culture, the Peninsula Woodland culture predominated, followed by the Laronde culture.

The native cultures who once camped along the beaches of La Cloche became increasingly advanced. Flint soon replaced quartzite. The Copper Indians, who mined the metal by bone chisel or heat, lived in harmony with other local people. Pottery changed from rounded clay to flared-rim pots. Dwellings changed from circular bark structures to sapling wigwams, and finally to palisaded villages of rectangular homes. Even burial practices changed, with burial mounds rejected in favour of elaborate platforms erected above the rocky ground.

From these prehistoric cultures came the Amerindian people known as the Ottawa, members of the Ojibwa Nation.

Indian Rock located at the mouth of Covered Portage Cove in Killarney Bay

Vision Quests And Rum Spirits

To the Ojibwa the magical mountains of La Cloche were a land of spirits: a land where braves, after fasting in solitude for days, would be granted their guardian angel from the spirit world; a land where the great Manitou dwelled in an underwater den; a land that was home to the Indian god Nanibozho; a land guarded by the raven; a land where shamans marked the rocks with paintings of the great thunderbird. It was land the Ojibwa Nation truly believed to be "Heaven's Gate."

In 1615, while travelling between the French River and La Cloche, explorer Samuel de Champlain met an Algonquin tribe later to be called the Ottawa. Tribe members were drying blueberries for the long winter ahead. The women wore breechcloths and the men's naked bodies were adorned with colourful paint and tattoos inscribed permanently into their skin by slash scars infected by charcoal and dye. Their ears and nostrils were decorated with beads, and their hair was gathered up on their heads in a unique manner. Champlain noted that the Indians' elegant hairstyle outdid the grand styles worn by gentlemen of the French court, and he decided to call these Indians *Cheveux-Relevés* ("the Indians with their hair raised up").

In his testimony in *Jesuit Relations* for 1640, Father Vimont stated, "To the south of these [the Beaver Indians, who lived at or near modern Beaverstone] is an island in the freshwater sea [Lake Huron] about thirty leagues long, inhabited by the Outaouan. These are people who have come from the nation of the 'raised hair.' "

At this time the "Raised-hair" Indians were at war with the Mascoutins (Fire Nation), an Algonquin tribe occupying the western shore of Lake Michigan. For weapons they used bows and arrows, and clubs. Moose-hide shields deflected enemy arrows.

The Huron word for the Upper Algonquins, who inhabited La Cloche and neighbouring Manitoulin Island, was "Ondataouat" or Ottawa, meaning "the people of the woods." The French half-breeds and voyageurs called the Ottawa "short-eared Indians."

The Ottawa, who hunted, fished, quarried quartzite, and picked blueberries, cranberries and wild rice in the La Cloche area, stabilized their main population on the neighbouring island. The Huron called this island "Ekaentoton," meaning "where there are very many things washed up on the shore." The French missionaries named it Ile Sainte-Marie, St. Mary's Island. For three centuries the Algonquins had been calling the island a corruption of Manitowaning or Manitowaling, which means "at the Manitou's den" or "where the Manitou dwells." Legend has it that there exists a subterranean passage between Manitowaning Bay and South Bay. It was believed that Manitou (the great Indian spirit) entered and made his way from one bay to the other by means of this passage.

To the Ojibway the mist-covered ridges of La Cloche were home to many spirits, a place they truly believed to be "Heaven's Gate."

The natives of the area were soon caught up in the European fur trade. They used skins to barter with the French for blankets, traps, guns and trinkets. To keep the Indians in alliance, the French presented them with gifts of brass kettles, colourful beads and cloth. And when the Indians' hunger for European goods waned, the French made sure they would continue to bring furs by creating a new appetite — a taste for rum.

European missionaries ventured out among the "savages" to spread the word of God. In 1649, while Father Jean de Brebeuf and Father Gabriel Lalemant were being tortured and killed by the Iroquois, Lalemant's cousin, Father Poncet, the first missionary on Manitoulin, was wintering on the island. A letter he wrote on May 18 clearly states his feelings regarding his appointment: "It was God's will to make me do penance for my sins during nigh on the seven months among these savages, companions of the life I was leading, and grant me the consolation of sending some of them to heaven . . . ."

In the meantime the Hurons were fleeing from the Iroquois and taking advantage of such hideaways as Manitoulin Island. But the moment news came of a great migration to a new settlement on the Island of Orleans, the Hurons joined up with the vast movement of canoes already on their way to the safe isle. The Ottawa remained, making up three tribes: the Kiskagons, the Sinagos, and the Keenoshe, or Pikes.

Father Louis André of Sault Ste. Marie was placed in charge of the faith of all neighbouring Indians, including those of Manitoulin and La Cloche. He spoke of his experience in *Jesuit Relations*: "I know not what my predecessors may have suffered in their country, but I proved well enough by experience how far one can go without dying of hunger. My daily allowance of food was not given me until after sunset; and if there were any bad morsel it was so small in quantity as hardly to suffice for sustaining life. To such straits [we] were reduced by ill success in fishing and hunting that year."

Father André survived by eating his moccasins and the bindings of his books, and continued educating his "savages" with the word of God. The mission still exists on Manitoulin. It housed the Jesuits until a permanent church was constructed in the town of Killarney in the early 1900s.

Today the native people of the Killarney area commonly believe in one God instead of many. Their lives have been drastically altered as a result of Champlain's meeting with the *Cheveux-Relevés*. But the raven's call still echoes through the land of Nanibozho and spirits still seep from the cracks of white rock.

Native Indians of the area ventured to exposed ridges, such as this one north of Nellie Lake, for their spiritual vision quests.

Voyageurs Of Shebahonaning

Etienne Brulé was known by his fellow adventurers as "Columbus of the Great Lakes" and as the "Immoral Scoundrel" by the priests who despised his constant womanizing. In 1615 he accompanied Champlain, and the two men were the first Europeans to travel the shores of the "sixth Great Lake," Georgian Bay, and witness the "white rock" of the North. Marquette and La Salle's journals also mentioned the white mountains they discovered while en route between Montreal and the western Great Lakes. It was not until the fall of Quebec in 1759, however, that this historic aquatic highway became a major travel route for the French fur traders called *voyageurs*.

These free-spirited men, employed by the North West Trading Company, paddled from the mouth of the French River into the "arms of Lake Huron," Georgian Bay. Brigades of up to 50 *canot de maître* (birchbark canoes 13 metres long and 2 metres wide) cut their way through the white-capped breakers which crashed against the 40-kilometre stretch of rugged shoreline, finally reaching Shebahonaning, a word of Algonquin origin meaning "safe canoe channel." Here the voyageurs could paddle protected from the high winds of the open bay.

At times even this watercourse would become rough, forcing the men to point their canoes inland, up the Mahzenazing or Chikanishing rivers, then portage their 4,000 kilograms of trade goods and hefty canoes over the La Cloche Mountain Range and back to the waters of the bay. Many actually preferred travelling overland, their stomachs and groins wrapped tightly to protect them from strangulated hernias, rather than battling waves powered by the evil spirits that dwelled beneath the waters. Joseph Delafield once noted, "It is fear . . . that in time of peril makes the voyageur the worst canoe-man possible. If overpowered by winds or waves, he instantly abandons his paddle or his oar and is worse than useless."

Shebahonaning was also a place of celebration for the hard-living men, for the La Cloche Mountains marked the halfway point on their 1,600-kilometre journey to Fort William, on the northern shore of Lake Superior. The men made camp among the boulders of white rock, and as the sun set behind the distant peaks, bannock was baked over the evening fire and dried meat was handed out. The canoes were turned upside-down, and if foul weather threatened, oil cloths were lashed to their sides. Under the light of torches the voyageurs repaired the freight canoes or circled the crackling embers and joined in song. These canoemen were known to work the whole day without eating, and to eat and sing the whole night without sleeping.

In 1790 a trading post was established at La Cloche. With the Indians increasing their traplines along the White-fish River and the voyageurs' canoes in constant need of repair after being dragged over the rough portages of the Mattawa—French River routes, the North West Company decided to set up permanent residence nearby.

In heavy competition, the Hudson's Bay Company wasted no time in becoming bothersome neighbours west of the stream which drained La Cloche Lake and the south of Post Hill.

When the two companies ended their quarrels and amalgamated in 1821, the new Hudson's Bay Company made Fort La Cloche the headquarters of the Lake Huron region. A former North West Company partner, John McBean, was retained as Chief Factor at La Cloche.

The post, located along a main travel route, was constantly short of food supplies, and simple pork and flour became the high-priced goods traded for the Indians' fur, maple sugar, corn and pumpkin. In fact, Fort La Cloche was so inferior to the other posts to the north that the Indians began to trade along the new nearby railway for handsomer goods, forcing the Hudson's Bay Company to close shop and sell their land to a timber firm in 1891, silencing the voyageurs' song in Shebahonaning.

Sunset on Killarney Bay: Once the hard-living men employed by the North West Trading Company reached the safe canoe channel called "Shebahonaning," they joined in song, for they had reached the halfway point on their trip to the northern shore of Lake Superior.

Storm-bound voya-
geurs made camp
along the granite
rock, at the mouth of
Chikanishing Creek,
before portaging
their 4,000 kilo-
grams of trade goods
and hefty canoes over
the La Cloche Moun-
tain Range and
back to the waters of
the bay.

The Town Of Killarney

Almost 200 years ago Etienne Augustin de la Morandiere set up his tent on the point of rocky shore where the quaint little town of Killarney now stands. At that time it was the only point of land which was clear of brush. Today Killarney is a thriving community whose docks harbour rustic old fishing boats and elaborate yachts.

Born in Varennes, Quebec, in 1767, Etienne de la Morandiere was a descendant of Robert de la Morandiere, who had come to live in New France in 1690. Leaving his widowed mother when he was 17, Etienne found his first job as a clerk and fur trader for the North American Fur Company. His business took him to many parts of the United States, and he eventually settled in Kalamazoo, Michigan, where he married an Ottawa Nation girl named Josephite Sai-sai-go-no-kwe (the Women of the Falling Snow) from Mackinaw. She was the niece and adopted daughter of Chief Kitchi Bashigigan (Big Gun) and a close relative of the famous Shawnee Chief Tecumseh. Etienne's Indian nickname was Wegibirge, meaning "writer," as he was constantly scribbling in his account book.

He was forced to leave his beloved family with the outbreak of the War of 1812. During the war he served as an ensign in the British forces, and for his diligent service he was later awarded 400 acres of land near Penetanguishene. The former businessman declined the offer, however, and returned to fur trading, opening up a substantial trading post on Drummond Island in Michigan. His booming business came to a tragic end in 1817, when fire raged through his establishment while he was away visiting the native trappers on Flat Point.

By June 1820 he had made the decision to move the remainder of his possessions to a nearby encampment where the Indians came from the mountains to trade their furs.

Etienne Augustin's great-great-grandson, Teddy de la Morandiere, who owns Rouche Rouge Campground in Killarney, explained, "To make it easier for the Indians, who had to paddle up the channel by canoe to his camp on Whitefish Bay, my great-great-grandfather took his sailboat down to Killarney, or Shebahonaning, as it was called then, and built a store, then used his sailboat to deliver his furs."

By 1823 the founder of Shebahonaning's first settlement had planted potatoes and corn, and even sowed wheat. The next year he brought the first cattle over from Manitoulin Island in a bateau. The small trading post soon grew into a flourishing community. In 1834 Reverend J.B. Proulx gave the first mass in Etienne Augustin's house.

The 1869 Province of Ontario Gazette and Directory stated, "The village [Shebahonaning] is hemmed in by mountains on all sides. It has a convenient steamboat landing and a good Catholic Church. The population, numbering about 100, chiefly Indians and half-breeds, live chiefly by fishing and hunting. Agriculture is neglected except as regards the usual vegetables for domestic use."

In 1874 Lord and Lady Dufferin visited Shebahonaning during their tour of Ontario, and many townspeople assert that it was Lady Dufferin who changed the name of the town from Shebahonaning to Killarney, because the hills and lakes reminded her so much of the landscape near Killarney, Ireland. However, in one of Lady Dufferin's letters, she recounts: "Thursday, July 30th., we went to Killarney (the Indian name of the place signifies 'here is a channel') and sailed by narrow passages to reach it. The Indians were collected on the wharf, and fired a salute. One of them made a speech to His Ex., stopping at the end of each sentence to have it translated into English. D.'s reply went through the same process. We spoke to the women and looked at the church, and distributed knives, pipes, tobacco and beads. There was one funny old man with a drum, who took to dancing and singing before us."

As the letter clearly points out, Lady Dufferin already thought of the village as Killarney before her arrival.

It is believed by others that merchant Robert Johnston had the town's name changed to Killarney between 1840 and 1850, when the name Killarney was considered by many newly formed towns. An 1848 stamp from the town's post office verifies that the name was changed before Lady Dufferin's visit, for the stamp had both Shebahonaning and Killarney printed on it.

Sportsman's Inn, 1899. – Ministry of Natural Resources

Port Of Call

The voyageurs' canoes, which once fought so hard against the wind and waves of Georgian Bay, were soon replaced by masted schooners and steel-hulled steamers — the latter having the better odds when pitted against the legendary gales of the great freshwater sea.

The first steamship to travel the mighty waters of Georgian Bay arrived in Killarney's port in 1836. The captain noted in the ship's journal: "We turned a point and . . . beheld a large assembly of Indians and well-dressed Canadians drawn out to see us. Two or three volleys were fired, and soon our lines were made fast; they hastened aboard to shake the hands of the adventurers. This was a trading post, the first we had any of us seen, and a few drams amply repaid the Indians for the expenditure of their ammunition. In the first evening we were invited to the house of the trader, Mr. Lamarandunt, and danced away to the merry sound of the fiddle, with the gay and lively half-breeds."

With the small town of Killarney increasingly becoming a major port of call, its neighbouring bays, inlets and isolated islands accumulated tales of the North Channel's toll of intrepid sailors and the rocky graves of their ghost ships.

The Dog Islands, for example, derive their name from an incident involving the Boyter family. The Boyters were sailing from Gore Bay to Little Current when bad weather struck and forced them to seek shelter for several days in a cluster of small islands. It was so cold that Mr. Boyter's legs froze and later had to be amputated at the knees. When the family ran out of food, they were forced to kill their pet dog and eat it, saving them from starvation and giving the islands their name.

One of the most memorable tales of the North Channel involves the British transfer of garrison from Drummond Island to Penetanguishene in 1828. As the story goes, a second vessel, the schooner *Hackett*, was required to help the brig *Wellington* ship men and supplies from the island to Penetang. The *Hackett*'s cargo consisted of a detachment of soldiers, some military goods, horses, cows, sheep, hogs, a French-Canadian named Lepine, his wife and infant child, a tavern-keeper named Frazer, and his 13 barrels of whisky.

During the trip, a storm brewed while captain, crew and many of the soldiers were helping themselves to the tavern-keeper's supplies. The vessel was driven onto the rocks bordering Horse Island while the men staggered drunkenly below deck.

The intoxicated passengers and crew reached the safety of shore, along with one horse, some pork, and the barrels of whisky. Mrs. Lepine and her infant were somehow forgotten aboard the wreck, while Mr. Lepine continued to entertain himself to an advanced stage of drunkenness.

During the furious storm Mrs. Lepine tied herself to the schooner's mast with her baby strapped on her back in a warm blanket. The storm continued throughout the night, lashing the exposed woman and her child with high winds and drenching rain.

In the morning, when the storm had subsided and the men had recovered from their drunken stupor, Mrs. Lepine and her baby were rescued by means of a yawl. The schooner's cannon had been pitched clean through the hull. Both the vessel and the Lepines' marriage were rendered a total wreck. The horse was left on the island, where it later died, giving the rock outcrop its name. The tavern-keeper took his remaining whisky and opened up a new business in Penetanguishene. And the Lepines' child lived to marry among later settlers (it's my guess to a non-drinker).

Steel-hulled steamers like the Manitoulin *(shown here in Killarney) soon replaced the birchbark canoes of the voyageurs.*

*Winter on Little
Sheguiandah Lake.*

Frozen In Time

During the long winter months, the townspeople of Killarney would sometimes venture out across the ice or over the wind-swept mountains to Little Current, Gore Bay, Manitowaning, Wikwemikong or even Whitefish to visit friends, pick up supplies, or just to challenge neighbouring towns to a game of hockey. Many of these journeys ended tragically.

A story by Pierre Regis de la Morandiere of Killarney, first published in the *Recorder* in 1912, tells of two men who lost their way on the frozen bay in 1863.

Ferdinand Proulx and Albert Moss left Killarney early on the morning of December 31, heading for Manitowaning Bay. A northwest wind brought a snowstorm that afternoon, forcing the two men to make a visit to Sam Solomon's place on Rat Island, where they were invited to stay the night.

New Year's Day brought more wind and snow to the frozen land, and Solomon, concerned that his guests might lose their way on the ice, asked the young men to remain at his home until the storm calmed. But Proulx and Moss assured their host that they had a good compass to guide them, and they went on their way.

Shortly after they left Rat Island, the wind shifted to the west and became a freezing 96-kilometre-an-hour gale. Unable to find their way back, the men wandered blindly through the storm, which lasted four full days. They searched in vain for any sign of the old Indian trail leading from Rabbit Island to Manitowaning.

The two men then continued along the shoreline, where Proulx, for some unknown reason, abandoned his snowshoes. They eventually started back for Rabbit Island, but huge balls of ice formed on their clothing, making it impossible to walk upright. Proulx and Moss crawled through the snow and freezing slush until they finally froze in their tracks.

Their bodies were found on January 5 by William Madweyosk, who was on his way to pay his annual New Year's visit to his father-in-law. He discovered Moss and Proulx's dog just a short distance north of Rabbit Island, then found Proulx himself frozen to death halfway between Rabbit and Rat islands. The stiff bodies were chipped from the ice and pulled on a sleigh to Sam Solomon's.

The task of delivering the mail for the North Shore by dog or pony during late fall or early spring had to be one of the most treacherous jobs around. Endless tales are told in Killarney of the mail carrier's hardships.

In 1872 two Wikwemikong Indians, Beaubien and his son-in-law Moses Ganewebi, were delivering the mail from the Soo to Penetang on a cold, stormy day in November. It wasn't until December, however, that Moses returned to tell his story. "I and my father-in-law were walking on the new ice, a few miles past Byng Inlet, intending to get ashore at a point further on. The wind was increasing from the northwest. We noticed that the ice had already moved several feet away and we could not get back to the land. I jumped in the water and swam ashore to a small island about an acre in size. My father-in-law laid the mail bags on the ice, sat down on them and, waving his hands to me, bid me goodbye forever, with compliments for his friends of Shebahonaning and Wikwemikong. As the ice was drifting past, poor Beaubien was soon lost out of sight. I remained on the island for two days and two nights without food or fire, tramping and running all the time to keep from freezing. At last some new ice formed, and with the help of two poles, I crawled on my hands and knees to the mainland, and reached Byng Inlet, where I was well taken care of for a few days, and here I am."

The following year two more Indian mail carriers, Little George and Isaac Jawana, met with mishap while delivering mail to Sault Ste. Marie. A severe gale mixed with snow and sleet suddenly came upon them about ten miles from Byng Inlet. The Indians' boat was overturned, tossing the men and their mail bags into the freezing water. The faithful mail carriers could save only two of the ten mail bags, one for Bruce Mines and the other for Byng Inlet, which they delivered in person that evening when they drifted to shore.

In November 1947 daily mail service was put on a year-round schedule by Norm Beavais. Tugs were still used for summer delivery and men still crossed the dangerous ice during the winter. Despite more frequent mail delivery, Killarney remained an isolated place with few amenities or services.

Aunt Nancy, Killarney's angel of mercy, brought no fewer than 500 babies into the world. She also doctored the sick and injured, and even buried the dead. This town, bordered by rugged mountains and a vast fresh-water sea, managed to survive its early years of isolation because of the determination and benevolence of true characters like Aunt Nancy. Once, on the way to visit an Indian woman who was having a baby in Beaverstone Bay, Aunt Nancy, Father Paquin and their dog team broke

through the ice just before they touched shore. They were pulled out by an Indian who spotted them thrashing about in the freezing water. Aunt Nancy later wrote of the incident: "When we got in the cabin, Father Paquin, who was getting on in years, was shivering something awful. I made him strip off all his clothes, including his long-handled underwear, and get into bed. The Indian and his family couldn't speak English and I tried to tell them that the good father needed dry clothes of some kind. Finally a giant of an Indian girl named Big Agnes produced a pair of her own huge bloomers and we had to put these on poor Father Paquin. They were as big as a tent, but Father Paquin didn't get pneumonia. And the baby arrived just fine!"

Regular twice-weekly air service between Killarney and Sudbury was not established until 1948. Hydro finally came to the town in 1951, greatly improving the area's quality of life. But a statement like that of Pierre Regis de la Morandiere still characterized Killarney residents' contact with the "real world": "I wanted to speak to a friend of mine who is a Frenchman, but I thought that a made-in-Canada phone wouldn't understand French, and I had to do my talking in English."

In 1962 Highway 637 reached the town from Highway 69. In celebration of the road's construction, the old tug that was used to deliver the mail on a regular basis was towed out into the channel and set aflame.

To a large degree, the road's completion was due to the persistence of Pierre Regis de la Morandiere, grandson of Killarney's founder. As the oldest citizen of the town in 1923, Pierre Regis travelled to Toronto to speak to the government in person concerning the road. During his visit the Toronto *Star* published a number of articles describing him as a "thick-set, sturdy man for his eighty years, with a great beard that he has worn practically all his mature life. It is greyish black and makes him appear almost as old as the hills of Killarney."

The newspaper made more of his unique character than Pierre Regis's actual quest. A *Star* reporter took him to Loew's Theatre and made note of the man's adventure: "It was the first time in his life that he had seen moving pictures. But the vaudeville acts came in for criticism. He claimed he could dance better than the bathing beauties, and he could teach the Indian actors some Indian songs to take place of the American ones.

"He is altogether not in favour of prohibition, as it deprives him of his joys of life, and he thinks money is well spent when invested in good whisky which is sanely used."

The reporter did state, however, that "P.R. does not think much of the Dury government, as it has done nothing for his district."

Thirty-nine years later Killarney got its road and tourists from Toronto flocked to the small, out-of-the-way town to witness for themselves characters in the mold of Pierre Regis.

After being reconstructed several times, the Sportsman's Inn still attracts tourists year-round. – Ministry of Natural Resources

Fishing The Bay

Although Killarney's early growth was due to agriculture, this lakeshore village also prospered from the fortunes that lay within the depths of the bay. Many farmers gave up trying to grow wheat and potatoes from rocky soil and replaced their hoes and ploughs with fishing nets and boats, reaping the harvest of Georgian Bay's fertile shoals.

Author Henry J. Woodside characterized the life of Georgian Bay's fishermen in 1893: "The fishermen receive from thirty to thirty-five dollars per month wages or, if paid by the weight, two-and-a-half to three cents per pound for fish, which, after passing through several hands and incurring heavy freight charges, are retailed at from eight to ten cents per pound in the cities where they are marketed. The fishermen are principally French. They are hardy, jolly, generous people, with splendid constitutions and able to make light of the hardships of their occupation. They are usually away from their families all summer months, and they rough it at the various fishing stations where a log shanty or tent is their shelter."

Obviously a man would have better luck striking it rich by panning for gold in the Klondike than by netting schools of fish in Georgian Bay, but the odd captain did find his fortune. J.P. MacDonald, for instance, built his business of five steamers from a small sailboat he fished from when he was only 13. MacDonald became the richest man in Blind River by catching 90 kilograms of walleye to each lift. In just three days he made himself $4,000.

In the late 1800s, however, the bay started to show signs of over-fishing. Angus Matthewman stated in 1893, "I have seen six and seven nets catch more fish in 1886 than are caught with thirty-five nets in 1893. The falling off is very great. This is caused by over-fishing, taking the young fish, and taking them when spawning."

At Killarney, in 1892, private fishermen shipped 635 tonnes of fish to Buffalo alone before the season ended. Better fishing craft and the increase in expert fishermen were the main reasons behind the enlarged shipments. The reduced fish population also suffered from the predation of the sea lamprey.

The saw-log business in the area was a further calamity for the fishing industry. Large log rafts were towed to the United States by tugs, travelling only three kilometres per hour, with the logs constantly grinding together, so that all the bark rubbed off, settling on the nets and over the spawning grounds of the fish.

With the fish population still on the decline in the early 1900s, seasons were shortened and more money was put into hatcheries. But nature could not mend the wounds inflicted by man's rapacity and Killarney now boasts of only a few full-time fishing businesses. The old tarpits, which once provided tar for coating the fishermen's nets, are visited only by tourists, and the faithful tugs have been left to rot along secluded shorelines. In less than a century Killarney's fertile shoals have become withered gardens of the bay.

The Shantyman's Axe

Alexander Murray noted the forest cover in the La Cloche area in his 1856 survey north of Lake Panache: "Pine grows abundantly of both the red and white varieties, and the white pine is frequently of large size. On the north side of Round Lake . . . there is a considerable extent of land yielding stout maple and oak, mixed with large-sized white pine."

By the 1860s loggers had found Murray's pine and had set up a number of lumber companies, mainly at Baie Fine and Collins Inlet, to prepare their timber for shipment aboard the Georgian Bay schooners.

Commonly known as "The Pool," Baie Fine supported at least four companies: the Spanish River Company logged from 1880 to 1927, except for the season of 1916-17. Two camps operated per season, removing a total of 57,300,000 board feet of red and white pine, 3,500,000 feet of hemlock, and 40,000 feet of spruce, booming the logs out the bay to distant mills.

The most significant lumbering company was based at Collins Inlet, east of Killarney at the mouth of the Mahzenazing River. The Collins Inlet Lumber Company mill was erected in 1868 and the wood it produced was used mainly for fence pickets, laths for plastering, and wooden boxes for packaging vegetables, fruits and fish. Large three-masted schooners, including some that had been built right at the mill, shipped the lumber south of Georgian Bay to such Lake Huron ports as Sarnia and Goderich.

Logging camps were set up on a number of inland lakes, including Bush, Bell, Balsam, David and Great Mountain. The trees were cut during the winter months and placed on the frozen lakes. When the spring thaw arrived and the ice broke, the logs were flushed down the waterway. Dams built between lakes caused fluctuation in water levels. With maple and birch being much heavier than pine and hemlock, the hardwood would sink below the booms and massive logjams occurred. This wood-weight problem saved hardwood stands throughout the area.

Bothersome logjams were not the only reason for prime timber preservation in Killarney. John Bertram, President of Collins Inlet Lumber Company and member of the Commission on Forestry appointed by the Ontario government, foresaw Ontario's future in the lumber business. Bertram sat in the House of Commons from 1872 to 1878 and made suggestions ultimately adopted by the Ontario Legislature for the discontinuance of the towing of Canadian sawlogs to American mills. Bertram strongly believed that the high demands for timber, without reforestation, could have devastating effects on the province, and once in office, he stated, "It is time the Dominion and Provincial governments [gave] more care to their property. Forests are becoming of increasing importance, and the study of the part they play in the welfare of any nation should be encouraged. The time is long past when trees were looked upon as enemies, and they should be grown wherever considered the most profitable crop."

False Solomon's seal grows under the shade of mixed hardwood stands.

Cotton grass is found in scattered patches along Georgian Bay shoreline.

Sphagnum moss carpets moist conifer forests.

Old tree stumps, hidden within thick new growth, remain as evidence of past logging days in the area. The landscape of La Cloche varies from nearly barren quartzite to lush mixed woodland.

In 1904 John Bertram died, the Collins Inlet Lumber Company mill was burned to the ground in 1918, and with the absence of machinery due to World War I, the property was sold. Shortly afterward, the village fell into disrepair, the schooners were left to haunt underwater graves, and Collins Inlet became another ghost camp on the northern landscape.

Built in the late 1800s, this mill at Collins Inlet prepared timber from La Cloche for shipment aboard the Georgian Bay schooners. – Ministry of Natural Resources

The First Tourist

The first actual tourist to visit Killarney came in 1837. After wintering in Toronto Mrs. Anna Brownell Jameson, wife of the first Vice-Chancellor of Ontario's Court of Equity, Robert Sympson Jameson, began a two-month journey through the Great Lakes region, without her husband. The first month was spent in luxury, visiting the settled areas of Southern Ontario, but the second included an organized trip known as her "wild expedition." By sailboat, bateau and canoe, Mrs. Jameson travelled the northern Great Lakes. Her journal, filled with impressions of the land and its people, was published in 1839 and was entitled *Winter Studies and Summer Rambles in Canada*. The following is an excerpt which notes her time spent travelling through the La Cloche area and her visit to the community of Shebahonaning (Killarney):

The voyageurs were disposed on the low wooden seats, suspended to the ribs of the canoe, except our Indian steersman, Martin, who, in a cotton shirt, arms bared to the shoulder, loose trousers, a scarlet sash, richly embroidered with beads, round his waist, and his long black hair waving, took his place in the stern, with a paddle twice as long as the others.

So much depends on the skill, dexterity, and intelligence of these steersmen, that they always have double pay. The other men were all picked men, Canadian half-breeds, young, well looking, full of glee and good nature, with untiring arms and more untiring lungs and spirits; a handkerchief twisted round the head, a shirt and a pair of trousers, with a gay sash, formed the prevalent costume.

About sunset we came to the hut of a fur-trader, whose name, I think, was Lemorandiere. It was on the shore of a beautiful channel running between the mainland and a large island. On a neighbouring point, Wai, sow, win, de, bay (The Yellow-head) and his people were building wigwams for the night. The appearance was most picturesque, particularly when the camp fires were lighted and the night came on. I cannot forget the figure of a squaw, as she stood, dark and tall, against the red flames, bending over a great black kettle, her blanket trailing behind her, her hair streaming on the night breeze — most like to one of the witches in Macbeth.

We supped here on excellent trout and whitefish, but the sandflies and mosquitoes were horridly tormenting; the former, which are so diminutive as to be scarcely visible, were by far worst. We were off the next morning by daylight, the Yellowhead's people discharging their rifles by way of salute.

. . . at last we perceived in the east the high ridge called the mountains of La Cloche. They are really respectable hills in this level country, but hardly mountains: they are all of lime-stone (?), and partially clothed in wood. All this coast is very rocky and barren; but is said to be rich in mineral productions. About five in the evening we landed at La Cloche.

Here we found the first and only signs of civilized society during our voyage. The North-West Company has an important station here.

The place derives its name from a large rock, which they say, being struck, vibrates like a bell. But I had no opportunity of trying the experiment, therefore cannot tell how this may be. (Alexander) Henry, however, mentions this phenomenon. Just after sunset, we reached one of the most enchanting of these enchanting or enchanted isles. It rose sloping from the shore in successive ledges of picturesque rocks, all fringed with trees and bushes, and clothed in many places with species of gray lichen, nearly a foot deep . . . .

These "respectable hills" of La Cloche continued to draw tourists long after Mrs. Jameson's visit. Schooners, which were called to pick up lumber from the neighbouring mills, defrayed their costs by bringing along paying passengers. Soon steamers travelling between Georgian Bay and Sault Ste. Marie made Killarney a regular stopover, laying the foundation for the tourist trade in the area. Accommodations were built for the sportsmen who came after hearing tales of monster muskie and gigantic moose. Some stayed at the Rock House Inn, others roomed at the Sportsman's Inn. The Killarney Mountain Lodge was the first lodge operated by a company from the United States. It was used exclusively to entertain that company's clientele. Ed Salo from Sudbury had six loggers from Switzerland build Blue Mountain Lodge on Bell Lake in 1952, and the clubhouse, where guests of the Collins Inlet Lumber Company stayed, was made into the Mahzenazing River Lodge's main hotel after the mill shut down.

By the turn of the century Killarney's bays and inlets were a magnet for large yachts, most of them owned by well-to-do Americans. A 1929 cottage register from Baie Fine lists visits by the president of the Zenith Radio Corporation, the inventor of the outboard motor (Evinrude), and the founder of Toronto radio station CFRB. Gutzon Borglum, the sculptor of Mount Rushmore, and ex-mayor of Chicago Hale Thompson were regularly seen yachting within The Pool, a popular stopover for the 100-foot luxury crafts.

Tourism is still going strong in Killarney. There are fewer tales of monster muskie and it is said that the moose are getting smaller, but the beauty of the "respectable hills" remains, and most importantly, so does the unique character of Killarney and its people.

View of Killarney Ridge from George Lake campground.

"*Nellie Lake*"

A.Y. Jackson 1882-1974
Hills, Killarney, Ontario
(Nellie Lake) c.1933
oil on canvas
77.3 x 81.7 cm
McMichael Canadian Art
Collection
Gift of Mr. S. Walter Stewart
1968.8.28

Present-day view of Nellie
Lake (renamed Carmichael
Pond) and Portage Saddle.

Artists In The Park

With its rolling hills, its lonely pines beaten by westerly winds, and its shimmering mountain lakes, Killarney is a true northern wilderness. This rugged landscape has always been a mecca for artists, but it was the Group of Seven who first exposed this painter's paradise. Searching for Canada's wild country so as to convey its beauty and environmental importance to the Canadian people, the Group arrived in the heart of La Cloche.

Four members of the group, Frank Carmichael, Arthur Lismer, A.Y. Jackson and A.J. Casson, worked throughout the area, hiking along its ridges and canoeing the chain of lakes and bays, all the while transferring the spirit of the land onto their sketch pads.

Frank Carmichael was the first member of the Group to set his sights on the quartzite hills. His brother-in-law, E.R. Went (Uncle Willy), discovered the beautiful area while working for INCO and told Carmichael he just had to see it. Carmichael was hesitant to take his brother-in-law's advice, feeling that a true artist should never be told where to find his inspiration. But in 1926 Carmichael finally visited Uncle Willy near Whitefish Falls, and from the fire tower on Tower Hill he viewed the hills and islands, falling in love with them instantly.

In 1934 Carmichael built a cabin on the beach at Cranberry Lake. The artist's daily routine consisted of rising at the crack of dawn, having breakfast, and then heading out to the neighbouring ridges to sketch. He would return by noon and would sometimes go out again, this time with the entire family — his wife equipped with a good book, his daughter with a pail for blueberries, and he with his sketch pad. Carmichael's daughter, Mary Mastin, remembers the joy of the family's annual extended canoe trips: "We would fish in Murray, swim at Grace, and sometimes visit Mr. Jackson and his artist friends on Nellie. I'll never forget the time A.Y. stood beside a blazing fire — this was during the heat of the day — and he actually offered me a cup of hot tea. I thought the man was mad."

One of Carmichael's favourite campsites for sketching was on the west end of Grace Lake. He was fond of the southern ridge and the two hills at the eastern extremity, both overlooking Nellie Lake. He also liked to paint the many hidden waterfalls in the deep valleys between Cranberry and Grace, and Nellie and Murray lakes.

Carmichael's artistic expression was based on a panoramic view of the landscape. The Baie Fine ridge, the Bay of Islands area, and the North Channel gave him this perspective, as did "Old Baldy," an outcrop of quartzite which the artist's sketching companions dubbed Mt. Carmichael. It was on this particular ridge that he captured "Northern Tundra," an excellent portrayal of Killarney's rugged topography.

Arthur Lismer, whose focus was Georgian Bay in its entirety, visited the hills of La Cloche frequently. In 1927 he produced "Happy Isle" while sketching on McGregor Bay.

Lismer was dazzled by the landscape and made the following note: "Georgian Bay . . . thousands of islands,

Franklin Carmichael sketching at Grace Lake, October 1935. – Joachim Gauthier/McMichael Canadian Art Collection Archives

A recent photograph of Frank Carmichael's sketching sites on the south ridge of Grace Lake.

little and big, some of them mere rocks just breaking the surface of the Bay — others with great high rocks tumbled in confused masses and crowned with leaning pines, turned away in ragged disarray from the west wind, presenting a strange pattern against the sky and water . . . Georgian Bay — the happy isles, all different, but bound together in a common unity of form, colour and design. It is a paradise for painters."

It was Lismer who introduced A.Y. Jackson to La Cloche when Jackson visited his cabin on Baie Fine in 1931. Jackson wrote in his autobiography, "Paddling around the islands and exploring intricate channels and bays that cut into the mainland provided me with much material."

One can visualize Jackson paddling along the shoreline, searching with keen sight for the subject matter that would best depict Canada's northland. In 1953 Lismer wrote of Jackson's environmental awareness, "His attitude toward the Canadian environment was that of a Northerner — born to explore the meaning of mountains, streams, woodlands, and lakes, and come to terms with them. Such is the nature of the English and Celtic strain and of Northern art . . . .

"Jackson's [works are] . . . easy to look at, disarming at first in their simplicity. In the hands of lesser [artists] they could be commonplace, but they also invite participation in the subtleties for his execution, of the thoughtful composition, and in the definitive mood. He gives the impression of an [artist] born to create background for others to occupy with any style, modern or otherwise, that the onlooker wishes, or is capable of projecting into them. He has true pioneer touch of setting the stage for the spectator to dream his own convictions and imagine other things. This is the time and space quality of his work."

Jackson sketched in McGregor Bay and on Grace, Gem and Nellie lakes. At the latter he painted "Nellie Lake" (actually Carmichael Lake, an attached western segment of Nellie).

Jackson was at home among the high ridges of quartzite, jumping from rock to rock or camping along the quiet shores of a secluded lake. In one of his letters, written after an adventurous day in the wilds of La Cloche, he noted, "The lake is like a sheet of glass and the moon, which has just risen over the hills, is sending a big silver shimmer over the water and straight into the tent."

In another letter he tells his niece of his stay at Grace Lake:

Grace Lake, no post office, no nothing. Oct. 22nd.
Dear Naomi:
Unky Punk is in his tent, with a tin pail full of cinders to keep him warm and a little candle to give him light, and some balsam boughs to sit on. Outside his tent the fire is crackling, it's a nice sound, you never feel quite alone with it . . . .
I merely make sketches. I have a box full of them. It's been hard work getting them with so much rain and cold wind. Grace Lake is surrounded with rocky hills. There are several little islands in it. Your Dad would love to spend a summer here. There is one little lake right up on top of the hills, with muskeg all around it, just full of pitcher plants.
I believe there are wolves and bears around, but they mind their own business, just like me. The mice are much more dangerous — I have to keep my grub hung up on the ridge pole of the tent. I feel them running over my sleeping bag at night, and I turn my flashlight on them and they go like hell.
Well, such is life at Grace Lake, my dear . . . .

A.J. Casson, the eighth member of the Group of Seven, produced a series of powerful paintings of La Cloche — "Rock Pool," "Cloche Hills," "Crescendo." The latter painting depicts a flock of storm-driven birds flying low over a barren landscape, representing the sense of solitude that he believed the area embodied.

Franklin Carmichael 1890-1945. Grace Lake *1933.*
watercolour and graphite on paper
29.2 x 33.8 cm
McMichael Canadian Art Collection
Purchase 1967
1967.1

Arthur Lismer 1885-1969. Pines Against the Sky *c.1929*
oil on panel
30.0 x 40.8 cm
McMichael Canadian Art Collection
Gift of the Founders, Robert and Signe McMichael
1966.16.106RV

Casson and his wife, Margaret, lodged at Birch Island in 1948. He was enticed to the area after viewing some slides of Picnic Island and Baie Fine.

Casson felt that one could easily "paint out" an area, but he always returned to La Cloche and continued to create some of his best work there. In an interview with Jon Butler, Casson said, "If I had my choice now, and at my age it's not easy to get to these places, that's the place [La Cloche] I'd want to go again.

"I don't think I ever got, anywhere, as much material as I did around La Cloche. You didn't have to hunt, you could get into one spot and work and work."

Casson went on many La Cloche sketching trips with Carmichael. He told reporters in 1984: "When Carmichael and I went camping, it was usually bad weather then in October. You can't use watercolours then because there is too much damp and rain. We'd take our sketch box with the colour in it, another box with panels in it, and a pencil pad and pencils and that's about all. You had to travel light."

After the deaths of Jackson and Carmichael, Casson petitioned the government to name lakes in the area for his painter friends. Jackson Lake is located just east of George Lake campground, and Carmichael Lake is at the west end of Nellie. Casson was given the same honour when Busky Lake, northwest of Murray, was changed to Casson Lake.

Besides the Group of Seven, many other well-known artists have visited the mountains of La Cloche and felt deeply attracted to this northern wilderness, including Carmichael's sketching companions Joashin Gauthier and Eric Aldwinkle. A.Y. Jackson partnered up with J.E.H. MacDonald, an artist whose work dealt with nature's delicate patterns. Robert Bateman painted "Grace Lake" and "Ravens in Killarney" early in his artistic career. The late Bill Mason, better known for his films than his work with a palate knife, enjoyed family outings and canoe trips throughout Killarney Provincial Park. Canadian composer

Harry Somers made his own artistic response to the white mountains in 1946 with his "Sketches for Orchestra" (with movements entitled "Horizon," "Shadows" and "West Wind"), and in 1948 with his "North Country" for strings.

Ross Bateman, Robert Bateman's brother, has conducted a number of art expeditions to Killarney with his high-school art class. After returning from a three-day canoe trip to O.S.A. Lake, having endured cold rain and heavy winds, the future artists used their sketch pads to express their feelings about the La Cloche hills. Some evoked dark textures of rock, the mist rolling off over the mountains after a rain, and the weathered pines along lonely island shores. Others, however, depicted less romantic experiences, such as being startled by a black bear along the portage, stepping in a fresh pile of beaver scat, and the cold, continuous rain.

Most of these young painters left the wilds of La Cloche infused with the same sense of awe and appreciation that the members of the Group of Seven felt when they first visited the area. Killarney is truly a painter's paradise.

Franklin Carmichael 1890-1945 La Cloche Silhouette 1939 McMichael Canadian Art Collection

A Park Is Born

The development of Killarney Provincial Park was facilitated by the Group of Seven's association with the area. On September 2, 1931, A.Y. Jackson was headed to Trout Lake (now O.S.A.) on a canoe and sketching expedition when he stopped at Baie Fine to chat with Mr. Spreadborough, a caretaker for the Spanish River Lumber Company. Spreadborough told "Hay Wire" (the caretaker's nickname for Jackson) that his employer was planning to log Trout Lake's shores. Jackson could not bear the thought of the lumber company removing the great pine along one of his favourite lakes.

Thirty-four years later Jackson recounted the incident in a letter to fellow artist and friend Eric Aldwinkle:

> I shall try to think back twenty years or more. I had been on a canoe trip with three professors, Dr. Barker Fairly, David Davis and Mr. Eaton of Ann Arbor.
>
> At that time the only way into Trout Lake [O.S.A.] was to make a four mile portage from Bay Finn [Baie Fine] on the Georgian Bay.
>
> Trout Lake is full of islands all surrounded by big quartz hills of the La Cloche range. There were a lot of big old pine trees there. We were told that the Spanish River Company were going to cut them all down the following winter. In Toronto, I spoke to a number of people to see if anything could be done to save the pines.
>
> Fred Brigden heard about it and came to see me. He said there was going to be a big convention in a few days of all the Natural History and similar societies from all over Ontario, and it would be a fine chance to bring the matter before them.
>
> At that time, I was rather shy and too scared to address a big meeting. So Fred suggested I should write a letter telling him about it. He would have it read to the convention. That was done and by good luck Mr. Finlayson the Minister of Lands and Forests was at the meeting. He went to see Fred and told him he could arrange with the Spanish River people to have an exchange of limits, which was done.
>
> So it was really due to Fred Brigden's efforts that Trout Lake became a park. Frank Carmichael probably had something to do with it being taken in trust by the Ontario Society of Artists.
>
> With best wishes,
> A.Y.J.

In the 1950s Canada's wilderness was disappearing at a drastic rate. The shantyman's axe was not totally to blame, however. Countless cottage sites were being purchased on Panache and Charlton lakes, and Whitefish and McGregor bays. One hundred and fourteen lodges lined the border of the North Georgian Bay Recreational Area and 500 hunting camps swallowed up huge chunks of wilderness areas within the reserve. To its credit, the government acted by increasing the number of provincial parks. K. Roberts of the Ministry of Lands and Forests took an interest in the Ontario Society of Artist's Killarney and in 1962 helped create the Killarney Recreational Reserve Act, halting land sales on 4,000 square miles of Great Lake shoreline. The Act was amended in 1964 and the North Georgian Bay Recreational Reserve was developed.

With Killarney now in the limelight, government officials began studying its potential. Golf courses, horseback-riding trails, and an elaborate downhill ski run and resort on Silver Peak were planned.

Three sites were proposed for the golf course, one being directly across from George Lake campground, running south along the east bank of the Chikanishing River. There was insufficient local interest in the proposal, however, and recent failures at French River, Sudbury and Sault Ste. Marie cancelled out the idea altogether.

The dream of an extensive park trail network for horse-back riding was exactly that, a dream, and it was soon placed on file for future consideration.

Silver Peak was believed to be a key potential skiing centre because there were no other sites in Ontario that could compete with its vertical drop, length of runs or lasting snow conditions. Ski pro Henry Moser made a survey of Silver Peak and said, "This could be developed into a better resort than Mt. Tremblant." But an extensive study showed that problems did exist. There was not enough soil to permit shaping of contours and the filling of lower sites; the limited usable ground area would only support a maximum of 800 skiers, not the several thousand originally estimated by consultants; the area could handle only one novice run, not a variety; restricted space would not permit mass movement of skiers from the central hill levels to the lower levels; and construction of roads from either George Lake or Carlyle Lake would be impossible because the mountains were in the way. So, in retrospect, the mountains of La Cloche saved themselves!

A committee considered a number of names for the new park, including Shebahonaning, Silver Mountains, White Mountains, Manitou Mountain, and White Rock, but it was agreed that the existing name, Killarney Provin-cial Park, was the most appropriate. It was further decided that the name Killarney Recreational Reserve conflicted with the park name, that the reserve's name did not effectively describe the location and size of the recreational reserve, and that the name of the reserve should be changed to "North Georgian Bay Recreational Reserve."

Much has changed since the zoning of the reserve and the development of Killarney Provincial Park in 1964. Back then Johnny Tyson acted as game warden, fire-warden, and the park's one-man maintenance crew. Today, even with several year-round, full-time staff members and a number of summer contract employees, management of Killarney's 48,000 hectares would be a nightmare if not for volunteer programs such as the Junior Rangers or the dedication of the Friends of Killarney Park.

The Junior Ranger program has been operated for years by Urban Hebert. Hebert enjoys taking *his* rangers into the interior of the park, and the young students enjoy his company, as well. Urben Hebert is a real-life Grizzly Adams. Once, on the Silhouette Hiking Trail, one of the boys in a work party accidentally cut his wrist on a bush-cutter. The boy looked solemnly into Hebert's eyes and asked, "Am I going to die?" "Of course you're not going to die," replied Hebert, and then he proceeded to carry the boy across the rugged terrain, over The Pig (the difficult portage between Threenarrows and The Pool) and down to Baie Fine, where an emergency boat was docked. He then took the boy to a nearby cottage owned by a nurse, where the young man's wrist was professionally bandaged.

Established in 1986, the Friends of Killarney is a non-profit charitable organization dedicated to furthering the educational and interpretive programs in Killarney Park. According to Past President Bert Treff, "The Friends of Killarney Park are committed to the enhancement of the wilderness experience for all its visitors, and they attempt to pursue this goal in co-operation with the Ministry of

Island campsite on O.S.A. Lake with Blue Ridge in the background.

Natural Resources, with park visitors, and with the residents of Killarney. Our aim is to contribute to the enjoyment and insight of each experience, as well as to ensure that environmental and ecological concerns are given top priority. Presently the Friends publish the park map and various trail guides. They are also beginning to find ways to enhance the benefits of the park for the people of Killarney — for over one hundred and fifty years the only custodians of this beautiful area."

Under the Killarney Provincial Park Management Plan, the park will continue to be classified as a "wilderness park," one of six in Ontario. With this classification the management of the park must adhere to guidelines set out by the Ontario Provincial Parks Planning and Management Policies and District Land Use Guidelines for Sudbury and Espanola — which means Killarney Provincial Park will not be jeopardized as Algonquin and Temagami provincial parks have been in the past. Present park management is striving for minimum human impact, so as to allow natural environmental processes and wildlife cycles to continue undisturbed. Under such management the park's natural resources will be protected and visitors will be encouraged not to overstay their welcome (overuse has been a major problem since the park's growth in popularity).

With Killarney being the closest wilderness park to a number of major urban centres, the Ministry of Natural Resources believes that the park's main contribution in the provincial parks system is the role of introducing visitors to their first real taste of a largely undeveloped natural landscape. Killarney is by Ministry definition "a threshold wilderness park."

John McGrath, Superintendent of Killarney Park since 1988 and an optimistic heel-biter, says of his domain, "There are a lot of areas where you can do what ever the hell you want, all that Crown land and other provincial parks. But we want to treat this little chunk as special. My definition of wilderness, keeping it simple in my mind, is a natural area where you can be by yourself. And we have that. I'll argue 'wilderness park' until I'm blue in the face, because that's what is basically saving Killarney Provincial Park — plain and simple!"

With strong views such as Park Superintendent John McGrath's, Killarney will remain Ontario's crown jewel.

Silver Lake. The moment the ice melts away from Killarney's lakes, canoeists head into the park's interior.

44

Breaking Camp

Though I have made many trips into Killarney's wilds, hiking its seemingly endless ridges and paddling its chain of lakes, the most magical spot to me, the one which characterizes the heart of the La Cloche interior, is not found in the seclusion of the northern range or the isolation of a windy bay, but rather among the crowded islands of O.S.A. Lake. To me, this small lake epitomizes the "true wilderness" that thousands of city-dwelling campers take home in memory to help them survive civilization.

My last trip into Killarney's interior was in the early fall. As the bow of my canoe broke the waters of O.S.A., the turquoise surface reflected the image of the shoreline. All around me bald outcrops of rock jutted into the clear water, lush juniper and blueberry shrubs surrounded the bases of weathered old pines, and of course there were brightly coloured tents, canoe bottoms and towels flapping on campsite clotheslines.

I continued down the lake most of the morning, trying to find the perfect site at which to make camp — something with a neck of pines to protect me from the wind, but still enough out in the open to snag a breeze and keep the summer's remaining mosquitoes at bay. The point of rock should face west-southwest to catch the morning sun at its tip and also the last rays as they sink behind the opposite shore. And the most important requirement on the checklist: the site must be unoccupied.

I was lucky enough to find what I was looking for on the third island coming in from the east. The last occu-

pants had kindly placed a stack of dried kindling beside the fire pit and there was even a comfortable log situated beside the fire. Everything was set.

With my coffee pot hanging over the coals, I watched the parade of canoeists paddling toward the nearby islands to make camp for the night: the disappointed fishermen, puzzled because "a lake so clean just has to have fish"; the older couple with the yappy poodle who refused to sit still in the canoe; the excited camp kids straining to synchronize their paddle strokes; the teenagers wearing rock-band T-shirts; and finally the college-age lovers who probably couldn't care where they pitched their tent.

At dusk O.S.A.'s rush-hour traffic subsided and darkness gradually blackened out the brightly coloured tents cluttering the opposite shore. As night set in, the illusion of wilderness solitude prevailed. Sitting by the water's edge, looking across the lake at my neighbours' campfires as they burned down to glowing embers then finally expired, I felt the backwoods closing in. The sound of a distant loon and the sharpness of the stars shining overhead I'm sure made each of us feel we were alone with nature.

Then there came the brief flashing of lights from an airplane flying overhead and the far-off sound of the Badgeley Island quarry blasting quartzite from the ancient hills. I felt like I was a kid again, sleeping in my tent in the backyard. The safety of the house may have been less than six metres away, but I still imagined wild animals wandering around my flimsy nylon dwelling.

The next morning I watched everybody break camp and pack their canoes for the trip out to George Lake. In just a few hours the weekend adventure would be over and the reality of the city's daily grind would return once more. The only thing left would be the stories of how rough but enjoyable it was out in the "bush."

As I watched the unlucky fishermen, the old couple who were still having problems with Fi-Fi, the exhausted camp kids, the teenagers, and the young lovers, I grew increasingly thankful for this not-so-wild wilderness we had shared. Each passing canoeist waved a cheery hello and wished me a good morning. Every one of us had different reasons for coming to the islands of O.S.A., but we all had in common a love and respect for the landscape.

Before pushing my canoe away from shore, I searched the well-used campsite for the forgotten tent peg, the ball of shiny tinfoil or the inconspicuous twist-tie. I wanted to keep the camp just the way I had found it.

The clear waters of O.S.A. may not be surrounded by hundreds of kilometres of untouched forest but, speaking for all the campers with whom I shared that weekend wilderness, I can guarantee that this beautiful lake and its islands provide nature enough to satisfy the soul.

Evening fire on Murray Lake.
"The conservation of waters, forest, mountains, and wildlife is far more than saving terrain. It is the conservation of the human spirit which is the goal . . . ."

Sigurd F. Olson (1976)

Take A Hike

Trekking over the quartzite ridges of La Cloche can be extremely demanding at times. Hikers should be physically fit and experienced before attempting extensive trips through Killarney Provincial Park's rugged trail system. A good map and guidebook are important to have along, but compass skills can be essential, especially if travelling across long stretches of barren rock.

Before setting off on your adventure, please remember that Killarney is a wilderness park. Park rules and regulations are there for your safety and well-being. Extended trippers must obtain a camping permit before heading out; reservations can be made in advance by phoning the main park office. A steep penalty is handed out to anyone camping off designated sites, and to reduce impact on sites, parties of no more than six people are permitted.

The following are a number of suggested day routes and extended trips through Killarney's interior. More detailed information can be found in the *Killarney Provincial Park Hiking Trails* booklet prepared by the Ministry of Natural Resources and the Friends of Killarney Park. The park map, also produced by the Ministry and the Friends of Killarney, is a must for anyone attempting trails in the park. In addition, a number of day-trip brochures are available through the park's main office and the Friends of Killarney bookstore. The interpretive staff hold day hikes during the week and guides are available through Killarney Mountain Lodge and Killarney Outfitters.

I highly recommend creating your own day-trips to the east or west along the portions of the Silhouette Trail, as well as off-trail ridge hiking. Leaving the markers and well-worn paths behind to venture over the open quartzite hills of Killarney may well be the highlight of your stay in the park. Be sure to make frequent note of landmarks and to avoid areas where map contours run close together, indicating steep grades. Also, keep away from loose rocks and mind your step.

SILVER PEAK:

Travelling east along the extensive Silhouette Hiking Trail, one can enjoy a four-day trip to Silver Peak (including return time via the same route). From the top of this 539-metre peak, you can view almost the entire La Cloche Mountain Range, the wild Georgian Bay coastline and Rainbow Country, lying north of Manitoulin Island.

To reach Silver Peak, head northeast of George Lake campground along the marked trail. The path meanders over pink granite and white quartzite, through hemlock forest and pockets of gnarled birch, maple, oak and the occasional white pine.

The first lake you come across is Jackson Lake, named after A.Y. Jackson, one of the members of the Group of Seven. From the south shore of Jackson you can view the transition from granite to quartzite on Hawk Ridge (so named for its nesting red-tails), which rises up from the east end of George Lake. Organized group day hikes to

The Crack. This significant split in Killarney Ridge is a popular destination for cliff-climbers and avid hikers in the park.

Hawk Ridge are conducted by the park's interpretive staff throughout the summer.

Before you reach the shores of shallow Little Sheguiandah Lake you will by-pass the connecting Cranberry Bog loop. Sphagnum moss — which the natives used as their disposable diaper system — covers the soft, spongy ground to your right, while nature's sheer granite sculptures appear to your left.

The trail makes its way over a beaver dam, past Wagon Road Lake, into Freeland, past Sealey's Lake campsite and over yet another beaver dam at Kakakise Creek. It then continues up a steep slope marked by the odd cairn, and through rolling quartzite hills toward "The Crack." This impressive split in Killarney Ridge has attracted hundreds of cliff-climbers to its sheer walls, and has drawn even more amateur rock ramblers, who head here from George Lake campground on day hikes. From the top of this geological masterpiece, you can see Killarney and O.S.A. lakes to the north and the rugged Georgian Bay shoreline to the south.

Little Lake Superior and Proulx and Shingwak lakes hold even more beauty ahead, with their clear waters cupped in white quartzite. The path then drops back down to Kakakise Lake and up again to the rugged ridges bordering Heaven Lake, one of the highest bodies of water above sea level in Ontario. I have always enjoyed making camp for the first night on Heaven Lake, especially during spring, when the mist rolls in from Georgian Bay.

The second day is just as exhausting, and as unforgettable, as the first. The first body of water you pass is named Bunnyrabbit, for the shape of its shoreline. The next several kilometres take you along more high ridges with interconnecting pockets of hemlock forest. Keep your eye open for fresh signs of Ontario's largest land mammal, the moose, for this mixed woodland is a prime mating area. On one fall trip I had a difficult time locating the markers on the trail while making my way through this hemlock-dominated forest. Fresh snow blanketed the worn path, and a baffled bull moose persistently chased me off course, mistaking me for a rival.

Lunch is best prepared at Silver Lake before making your way toward Silver Peak. For one thing the water in this lake is considerably better than that found in the beaver ponds ahead. (Drinking pond water can cause beaver fever.)

Shortly after Silver Lake the trail turns left along an old logging road for approximately 1.5 kilometres. This section of trail, enveloped in brush and often muddy, makes a perfect breeding habitat for bloodthirsty mosquitoes, so make haste towards the Silver Peak turnoff.

The hike up takes a little over an hour. Don't lose vigour halfway up, for the view from the highest peak in the park is well worth your grueling efforts.

You can't camp on the summit of Silver Peak, so plan to climb back down and return to George Lake campground via the same route, possibly stopping at Silver Lake the second night, and Proulx or Sealey the third. Expect to hike double time heading back, in order to escape trekking through the darkness along the last section of the trail.

Silver Peak can also be reached in a single day by driving to Bell Lake access point, canoeing to its western inlet, and then taking the trail up to the peak. Canoes can be rented from Blue Mountain Lodge on Bell Lake. This is a long one-day trek, so prepare for it appropriately.

BAIE FINE:

Baie Fine can be reached in a day by hiking west along the Silhouette trail. Begin your journey by crossing the dam where the Chikanishing River flows from George Lake. Note the numerous charred tree stumps along the trail, evidence that the area was once cleared for a logging company tote road. Thickets of white birch, poplar and alder now grow in profusion atop the scarred surface.

Worn paths meander off to the right, heading toward George Lake, and to the left an unmaintained cross-country ski trail loops back to the campground.

After about half an hour you will reach the shore of Lumsden Lake, a crystal-clear "dead" lake which once held a large population of lake trout. Now it is impossible to locate even a single aquatic plant rooting itself in the acidic soil. (Lumsden was one of lakes hardest hit by acid rain. INCO has now raised the height of their smokestacks and some of the lakes have begun to recover, but now Quebec's sugar maple are in decline.) The ridge projecting from the south end of the lake is an excellent place to view Georgian Bay, and juicy blueberries grow in abundance along its sunburnt ledges.

From Lumsden the main trail works its way through mixed woodland, over a number of beaver ponds, then continues to Acid Lake. (The hike from Lumsden to Acid Lake and return via the same route is an excellent morning hike on its own.)

Trekking onward you will pass Cave Lake, Artist Creek, and head up toward the steepest portage in the park, between The Pool at Baie Fine, and Threenarrows Lake. The north ridge provides a spectacular view of this historic bay where yachts have anchored since well before the park was developed.

The trip takes the entire day, so don't plan to sunbathe for too long at Baie Fine before starting your hike back to George Lake campground.

THE SILHOUETTE TRAIL LOOP:

This trip takes 7 to 10 days and covers over 100 kilometres of Killarney's wild landscape. Named after Frank Carmichael's painting "La Cloche Silhouette," the trail is dedicated to the memory of the one member of the Group of Seven who captured the heart of La Cloche like no other. The *Killarney Provincial Park Hiking Trails* guidebook, prepared by the Ministry of Natural Resources and the Friends of Killarney Park, gives a detailed description of this extensive loop in five sections: Baie Fine, Threenarrows, Hansen Township, Silver Peak and Killarney Ridge.

I suggest a clockwise route, embarking westbound. Make sure to plan your campsites with the park staff, and try to stick to that plan, thus avoiding confusion regarding permits and reservations.

Once you have passed Baie Fine and clambered up the steep 1,530-metre portage to the old dam (built to raise water levels in three individual lakes to the north, creating one larger lake called The Threenarrows), the path works its way toward the north shore, crossing by way of Kirk Creek's south bank.

The trail finally eases off a bit and follows relatively flat terrain along the shore of Threenarrows. To the west lies an extensive marsh habitat alive with breeding insects and colourful birds. Another oasis for wildlife, Bodina Lake lies in the heart of Killarney, just 630 metres off the main trail. Surrounded by boreal conifers, this solitary setting is the perfect place for a peaceful slumber in the wilds of Killarney — unless you are a red squirrel and there is a hungry pine marten nearby.

After following the north shore of Threenarrows for a few kilometres, the trail leads up the Northern Range of the La Cloche Mountains. The terrain is rough going, but the views are breathtaking.

During past trips my path has been blocked by moose, deer, bears and even a bobcat. One particular October day, as I made haste through damp snow flurries, the quartzite ridges suddenly came alive with hundreds of snow buntings. My pace quickened and I prayed that I would make it out of the park before the approaching winter storm made these arctic finches feel more at home.

Hemlock forest dominates the landscape on the way to Moose Lake, opening up now and again to reveal excellent views of the Blue Ridge Range. This always gives me a sense of accomplishment, getting the chance to look back on the distance I have travelled and the rough

O.S.A. Lake and Killarney Lake from the La Cloche Silhouette Hiking Trail.

Spring hikers enjoy a warm fire at an interior campsite on Norway Lake.

Hikers traversing a creek flowing into Boundary Lake.

Hikers following rock cairns along open stretch of the La Cloche Silhouette Hiking Trail.

The western end of historic Collins Inlet.

terrain I have traversed. It also helps to push me onward, past Shigaug, Little Mountain Lake, and down towards David and Boundary lakes, where the open ridge tops transform into lowland brush and mixed hardwoods.

The trail then leads south and, about one kilometre later, divides to join both the old logging road and the path up to Silver Peak. If you're thinking about taking a side trip up to the summit, it takes about an hour. I highly recommend the extra trek, but make sure to allow time to make camp before the two-day journey southwest to George Lake campground.

GRANITE RIDGE TRAIL:

Located just across Highway 637 from George Lake campground gatehouse, this two-kilometre hike takes you on a tour of Killarney's historic past. It also features spectacular views of Georgian Bay, Collins Inlet and the La Cloche Mountains.

The pine plantation and open fields, which have been taken over by strawberry, hawkweed and hawthorn, were once the Tyson family homestead. This was the first farm in Killarney. The Tysons raised pigs, chickens and cattle, and grew hay, vegetables and fruit trees. A lightning storm destroyed the house in the late 1960s and only ruins of the log buildings and pieces of rusted machinery remain.

The trail leads toward the town of Killarney along what was once the Tysons' winter road. A late 1940s Dodge and a 1931 Chevrolet have been abandoned beside the path. These were once driven by Tyson's grandson, Billy Burke, the park ranger in the early years.

The trail soon forks. If you stay to the right you will climb a steep grade through sturdy hemlock and red and white pine. As you ascend the slope, the forest floor changes from rotten stumps, laden with trailing arbutus and bunchberry, to patches of blueberries and huckleberries, and lightning-burned old-growth pine covering the pink granite ridge.

Further along you reach the lookout point, which offers a tremendous view of Georgian Bay and the mouth of Collins Inlet. Phillip Edward Island is the large land mass to the south. You can also see Lonely Island and the much-nearer Squaw Island, once home to a fish-canning business. To the north the rugged La Cloche Mountains dominate the landscape, with their white ridges towering over the pink granite to the south, crowned with stands of red oak which have been stunted by intolerant weather conditions.

The trail heads back down toward the Tyson farm, making its way through lush white and yellow birch, sugar and mountain maple, and mature hemlock stands that somehow survived the shantyman's axe in the early 1900s.

The path passes through the old Tyson site once again before returning to the road across from George Lake campground's gatehouse, ending a perfect two-hour tour of Killarney's woodlands and panoramic vistas.

CHIKANISHING RIVER TRAIL:

This two-hour loop begins at the Chikanishing boat landing, located at the end of Chikanishing Road, three kilometres west of George Lake campground (just before the Bailey bridge). This historical hike takes you up and down the rugged granite of the Georgian Bay shoreline, where old boom rings are still embedded in the rock, and sharp-shinned and Cooper's hawks soar above the maple, birch and hemlock.

There's a perfect cotton-grass lunch spot along the shore of Georgian Bay where I once spotted a golden eagle making its way south above the wind-swept islands.

The first quarter of the trail provides photography buffs with a great opportunity to capture the setting sun as it drops behind the distant mountains and the bay, or the silhouettes of elegant yachts navigating the isolated coastline.

A series of plaques describes points of interest along the way, such as old voyageur and native campsites at the mouth of the Chikanishing or anchor sites for lumber ships of Killarney's logging era.

CRANBERRY BOG TRAIL:

An absolute paradise for bird-watchers, this trail meanders through a succession of marshes and bogs, most featuring the carnivorous pitcher plant and sundew, and wild cranberries, which the natives once harvested in the area. The route can be completed in two hours (even less if you happen to forget your bug repellent back at camp).

The four-kilometre trek begins on the east end of George Lake campground. Numbered stops are located along the way, with corresponding headings in the *Killarney Provincial Park Hiking Guide*, which can be picked up at the gatehouse.

Recently there has been a heightened public awareness of the need to preserve Ontario's wetlands. It wasn't long ago that society classified marshes, swamps and bogs as simply breeding grounds for bothersome insects. As you hike through this wildlife haven, you will soon realize that more than just bugs breed among the cat-tails and sedges.

The first wetland along which the trail passes is called Proulx Marsh. The vegetation here thrives in the nutrient-rich soil, even when water levels drop during the dry season. Bluejoint grass, which grows in abundance, fed Alex Proulx's cattle, but now provides a playground for the otters who visit the marsh frequently in the early morning.

Further on, you will notice a change from pink granite to the characteristic white quartzite of La Cloche. At one point along the trail you will actually step over the borderline of the two geological regions or provinces. The pink granite of the Grenville Province extends all the way to the coast of Labrador.

I can guarantee the beavers in the middle pond are free of headaches. Their main diet of poplar is well known for the medicinal component, acetylsalicylic acid (aspirin), contained in its inner bark. Birch and maple also grow in profusion in neighbouring stands, giving these ingenious rodents a smorgasbord of delectable trees. Being primarily nocturnal, the beaver ventures across the woodland under the cover of darkness to gather supplies for dam construction and the odd midnight snack. It is during this time that many fall prey to the coyotes and wolves in the area. However, accidental deaths occur more commonly than killings by predacious canines. Contrary to popular belief, beavers are not particularly skilled at lumbering. Many are crushed by the very trees they decide to fell.

The third body of water you come to differs from the previous two by its stagnant stench and lack of nutrients, causing plants to maroon themselves on islands or sphagnum mats. These decomposing layers of plant life, saturated by water, become extremely acid, and with the lack of oxygen slowing down decay, peat is formed. Pitcher plants and sundew feast off blackflies to supplement the few nutrients available in the soil, while leatherleaf, cranberry and stunted black spruce struggle for their existence. This organic gruel will swallow the unwary moose who is too lazy to walk around this boreal quicksand.

After following Cranberry Bog's northwest shore, the trail leads back into a mixed woodland of sugar and mountain maple and hemlock. A tremendous variety of birds can be found here: thrushes, wrens, nuthatches, woodpeckers, and of course the familiar chickadee. The odd tamarack, the only northern conifer that sheds its needles in the autumn and regains them in spring, appears in the dampened stands. These unique cone-bearing trees attract siskins, grosbeaks and one of the main predators to young birds in the nest, the red squirrel.

The route turns to the left on the Silhouette hiking trail, and then back to the main campground, rounding off an educational and entertaining walk through Killarney's wilds.

White pine along
Cranberry Bog trail.

*Canoeists on
Killarney Lake.*

Paddling The Park

When my canoeing companions and I gather round the fire and share stories of past Killarney trips, tales of unpleasant adventures usually outnumber those recounting fair weather and smooth paddling. We've crossed countless lakes, portaged over jagged quartzite and poled through thick, bug-infested bogs. Our arms have strained to battle the seemingly endless onslaught of wind and waves, and there have been stormy nights when we all feared that our flimsy nylon tent would become the next Noah's Ark.

Why then do we go? Quite simply, it's to become part of this wild landscape, to be invigorated by the spacious breadth of turquoise lakes and shimmering quartzite, and to bring home to our busy daily lives unforgettable memories.

The following are a number of suggested canoe routes within the interior of Killarney Provincial Park. These basic descriptions are not meant as definitive guides. Before heading out on any excursion in the park, make sure to purchase a detailed map showing campsites, portages and topography. Familiarize yourself, as well, with important points such as maximum site capacity and pre-registration permits for the interior, and be sure to follow the can and bottle ban. It is important to remember that canoe routes and campsite locations change over the years, so abide by the current No Camping signs and check your planned route with park staff before setting out.

For more information contact Killarney Provincial Park at (705) 287-2368.

ROUTE #1
George, Freeland, Killarney, O.S.A., return
Duration: 2 to 3 days

Because George Lake access point is the major launching site for a variety of canoe routes into Killarney Provincial Park, the sandy beach where you depart can be quite busy, but the entanglement of paddlers eventually spread themselves out.

George Lake is an excellent place to introduce visitors to the landscape of La Cloche. A drastic geological zone change becomes apparent the moment your canoe rounds the first bend of granite shoreline to your right, revealing an abrupt protrusion of quartzite intermixed with ancient, blackened volcanic sediment. Strong winds are almost constantly sucked in from either east or west; I can't remember a time canoeing on George Lake when the prevailing winds didn't battle my bow.

The first portage measures only 50 metres. However, it is highly advisable to plan a good half hour to fight the crowds of canoeists lined up waiting to use this extremely popular portage. The dam to your right was constructed by a lumber company in order to fluctuate water levels and was finally abandoned in 1916.

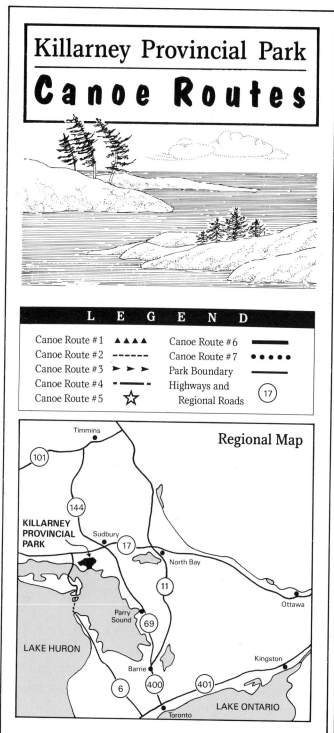

Killarney Provincial Park
Canoe Routes

LEGEND

Canoe Route #1 ▲▲▲▲	Canoe Route #6 ▬▬▬
Canoe Route #2 -------	Canoe Route #7 ••••
Canoe Route #3 ►►►	Park Boundary ▬▬
Canoe Route #4 ▬·▬·▬	Highways and
Canoe Route #5 ☆	Regional Roads ⑰

Regional Map

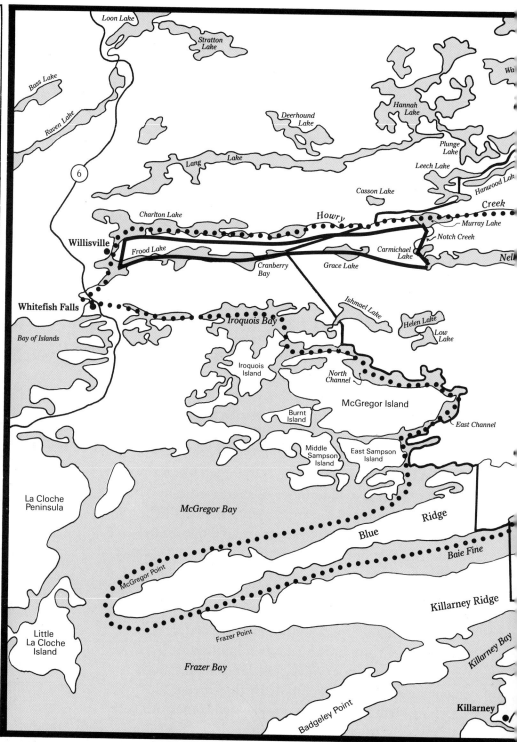

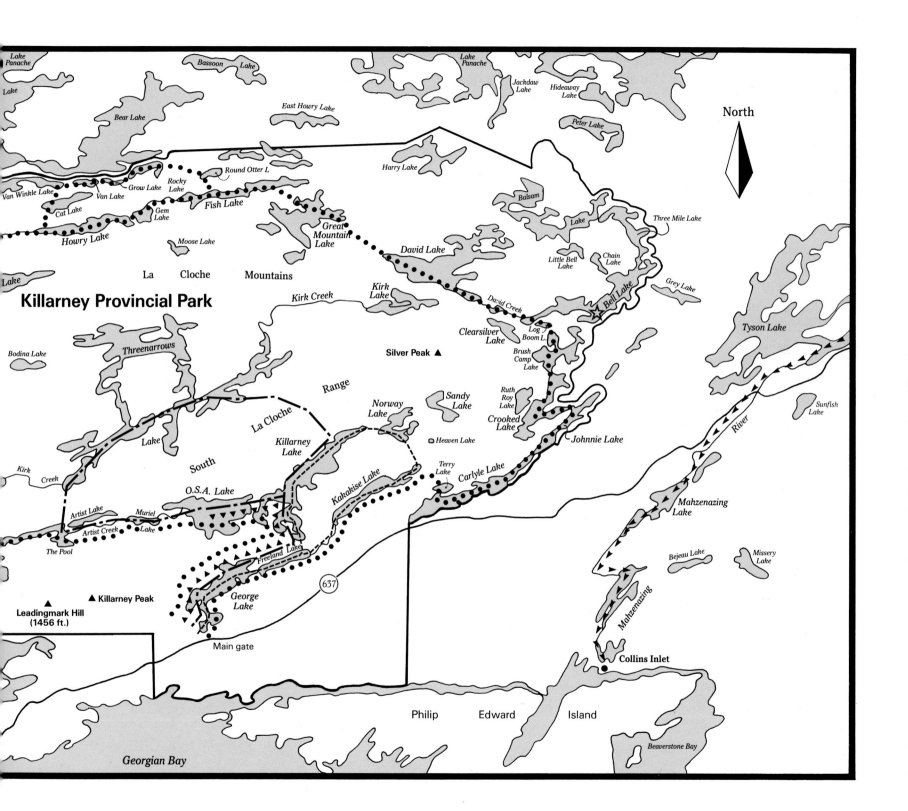

Killarney Provincial Park

North

Lake Panache

Bassoon Lake

East Howry Lake

Lake Panache

Jackdaw Lake

Hideaway Lake

Peter Lake

Bear Lake

Harry Lake

Three Mile Lake

Van Winkle Lake

Round Otter L.

Rocky Lake

Grow Lake

Van Lake

Balsam Lake

Cat Lake

Gem Lake

Fish Lake

Great Mountain Lake

David Lake

Little Bell Lake

Chain Lake

Grey Lake

Moose Lake

Howry Lake

La Cloche Mountains

Kirk Creek

Kirk Lake

Bell Lake

Tyson Lake

David Creek

Bodina Lake

Threenarrows

Silver Peak ▲

Clearsilver Lake

Log Boom L.

Brush Camp Lake

Range

Sandy Lake

Ruth Roy Lake

Lake

La Cloche

Norway Lake

Heaven Lake

Crooked Lake

Johnnie Lake

River

Sunfish Lake

Kirk Creek

South

Killarney Lake

Kakakise Lake

Terry Lake

Carlyle Lake

Mahzenazing Lake

O.S.A. Lake

Artist Lake

Muriel Lake

Bejeau Lake

Missery Lake

Artist Creek

The Pool

Freeland Lake

Mahzenazing

▲   ▲ Killarney Peak

Leadingmark Hill
(1456 ft.)

George Lake

(637)

Main gate

Collins Inlet

Philip   Edward   Island

Beaverstone Bay

Georgian Bay

The second lake, Freeland, is one of the last remaining "living" lakes in the area. Water lilies abound and extra effort is required to push your bow through the thick vegetation, where you are almost guaranteed to flush a flock of teal, a family of mergansers, or a lone heron. Rich in wildlife, this low-acid-level lake is a reminder of Killarney's past, when all the lakes in the area contained lush aquatic plant and animal life.

The portage into Killarney Lake is located to the northeast and covers 430 metres of relatively flat topography. The path leads through a mixed cover of "moose maple" (mountain maple), birch and pine, with a small stream trickling to the right. In the early days canoeists used a rugged portage, from the most northern bay of George Lake, over Killarney Ridge, to reach O.S.A. Lake. Because of the rough incline, the route was altered to go through Freeland and Killarney.

Killarney Lake, with its surface reflecting the sheer outcrop of white rock, is said to be a mirror image of a landscape near Killarney, Ireland. Many canoeists prefer to camp on this lake, making a day visit to O.S.A. before returning to George.

Loons populate a number of lakes in the park, but here, on Killarney Lake, there is always one or more of these prehistoric birds sounding a warning call to announce visitors paddling into the interior. Their mournful cries carry across the surface of the water and echo off the rocky shoreline.

To reach O.S.A., the most popular lake in the park, choose between a 180-metre portage, following a lift-over and a small pond, or a lengthy but more direct 500-metre portage through a maple stand where a ghost lumber camp has been swallowed up by brush. The local natives once came to collect maple sap in this collection of hardwoods. Willy Bernard, an old trapper from Killarney, claims that, according to legend, it was here that the great spirit Nanibozho grew angry over his people's greed concerning the precious syrup, which once flowed ready-to-use from the trees. To punish them, Nanibozho stood upon the neighbouring ridge and ordered the heavens to flush the trees with rain, transforming the syrup to sap and thus plaguing the people with the labour-intensive task of boiling out Nanibozho's spell.

O.S.A., known over the years as Trout Lake, Kendrick Lake and Whiterock Lake, is the actual birthplace of Killarney Provincial Park. It was here that Group of Seven painter A.Y. Jackson, with the help of a number of determined environmentalists, halted the Spanish River Lumber Company's plan to reap the benefits of their timber rights along the shore. In 1933 the Minister of Lands and Forests changed the lake's name to honour the dedication and efforts of the members of the Ontario Society of Artists (O.S.A.).

A number of island campsites are available, my favourite being the third from the east. Don't be fooled by the old wives' tale that island campsites are free of bears. One morning in late September while I was busy brewing coffee on the breakfast fire, a bear, matted and wet from his swim, toppled an old birch nearby and began tormenting the quivering grubs living inside. Less than 20 metres away, I was hoping and praying that the bothersome bruin wouldn't mistake *me* for a quivering grub.

From camp on O.S.A. one can proceed either along the ridges to the north and south or paddle west to Baie Fine for the day. There are no set trails heading up to the ridge tops; simply choose a spot where you can dock your canoe and commence climbing, taking note of landmarks in the neighbouring area so that you can easily locate your canoe on the return trip.

The quartzite ridge tops are spotted with stunted oak (providing excellent habitat for the local deer population), barren rock scarred by previous lightning strikes, and blackened water pools. Make sure to wear a hat and bring along plenty of water, the exposed ridges can become quite humid.

Morning sun and mist on O.S.A. Lake.

Canoeists heading into Killarney Provincial Park's interior by way of George Lake.

Plan an early start back to George Lake to beat the rush-hour traffic on the Freeland Lake portage and before the northwest wind whips up George Lake.

ROUTE #2
George, Freeland, Kakakise, Norway, Killarney, Freeland, George
Duration: 3 days

This route makes a perfect long-weekend trip into Killarney. It uses the same access point as Route 1 and takes you across George and Freeland lakes, then on to Kakakise Lake via the 970-metre portage starting at the southeast inlet of Freeland. If water levels permit, it's better to work your way to Kakakise over the series of beaver dams rather than shouldering all your equipment across the lengthy portage.

Kakakise Lake, which appeared on an 1895 forester's plan as Caughagese Lake, has both black granite and white quartzite along its shore. The point of rock protruding from the south, just as you exit the narrow peninsula, was once home to one of the many hunting cabins erected throughout La Cloche before the development of the park.

Some trippers prefer to camp the first night on Kakakise Lake, but I have always pushed on to Norway, leaving a large part of the paddling behind, thus allowing me to spend the next morning exploring the South La Cloche Range or hiking to Sandy Lake. The portage into Norway is a long, steady 1,560-metre climb that can slow one's pace to a crawl, especially on a hot summer's day. The incline doesn't seem obvious until three quarters of the way along, where the Silhouette hiking trail cuts across heading toward Heaven Lake.

If you decide to hike into Sandy Lake the next day, before moving on keep your eyes open for red-tails or broad-wing hawks soaring in the thermals above the ridge.

A small stream meanders down into Sandy Lake from the east. I once followed this trickle of water down into Sandy Lake from along the Silhouette hiking trail by Silver Lake. I was leading a group of high-school students on a hiking trip when we were forced off the trail by a build-up of spring snow and slush. Detouring through the thick brush, we set a compass bearing for Norway Lake, where we planned to make camp. I'll never forget one particular student who happened to sink up to his waist in a mixture of slush and muskeg mud along the creek. After pulling him out, we discovered that his left shoe had been swallowed by the earth. Several attempts were made to retrieve the shoe, but the student was eventually left to hike out of the park with one mud-caked sneaker and one very worn woollen sock.

You should be on your way again by mid-afternoon. The 1,420-metre portage into Killarney Lake (known by the locals as Sturgeon Lake) brings you deeper into the heart of the park. The steep quartzite cliffs of Killarney and the South Ridge create a sense of confinement, and one is easily humbled by this grand display of nature. Each paddle stroke takes you deeper into the remote, wild section of the La Cloche Mountain Range.

For the third and final night you can choose to camp at one of the various sites on the western end of the lake or go the extra mile and slip into O.S.A.

After the sun sets behind the distant hills, delay starting your campfire. Instead head down to the water's edge and catch the moon's rays reflecting off the shimmering lake and white quartzite. You may even be lucky enough to spot the northern lights dancing over the La Cloche Range. It's an unforgettable sight.

It should take only three hours to journey back to George Lake campground by way of Freeland Lake, allowing ample time to lie in your tent until the morning sun finally begins to burn through the thin nylon walls and starts to bake you inside your own sleeping bag. A leisurely breakfast and an even-paced paddle back to the campground should give you ample time to contemplate your return to civilization.

ROUTE #3
Tyson, Rock, Mahzenazing Lake/River, Collins Inlet
(main route)
Duration: 2 to 3 days

The ghost town of Collins Inlet is not situated in the park, but it is still well worth mentioning as a suggested canoe route in the area. It can be reached straight from the town of Killarney or from the Mahzenazing River south of Highway 637, but the main route used by canoe-ists starts from Tyson Lake north of Highway 637. This route is best planned for the spring, when water levels are much higher on the Mahzenazing River. Levels have fluc-tuated over the years due to logging dams.

Stunted pine, patches of "moose maple," and a mixed conifer and deciduous growth cover the ugly scars inflicted by past logging practices. The river's banks are lined with rock — layers upheaved, twisted, exposed or pressed smoothly along the shore. The river bottom frequently flashes under your canoe, dizzying and trans-fixing. At times, however, the river appears more like a lake, channeling through islands of rubble covered with alder and weather-beaten pine.

On past trips through the narrow section of the river before Collins Inlet, I've sighted numerous deer stepping across the rocks along the shore. The moment they sense my presence, their alarms sound, their ears twitch, noses snort, they stand immobilized for a brief second, then bound back into the woods.

Eventually the watercourse makes its way to a historical landscape where Indians painted ochre symbols on the rocks (one being a canoe with one of its occupants crowned with a cross, indicating a priest) just west of the river's mouth, along the north shore. Etienne Augustine de la Morandiere's clientele used the inlet en route to Killarney's trading post. Voyageurs paddled through to escape the weather and waves on Georgian Bay. And in 1868 a lumber mill was established here.

Bessie Pitt, a resident of Collins Inlet during its heyday, remembers her mother telling her the tale of how, as a delicate bride, she had travelled from Whitefish, over a chain of frozen lakes bordering the La Cloche Mountains, to their new home at the mill site: "In the end of January 1902, when there was an abundance of snow and wolves in the community, my mother, a city girl who came from a home with a parlour maid and cook, came fresh from her honeymoon in New York to the isolation of Collins Inlet. By horse and cutter they travelled across the lakes, bear rugs placed over their backs and a big pan at their feet with hot bricks in it to keep them warm. My mother said the horse would go down a bit in the slush and more or less scare her to death. They progressed nicely until they reached one of the camps on Brush Lake."

Fire destroyed the mill in 1917, causing Collins Inlet's decline. Other companies still worked out of the Mahzenazing, rafting gigantic booms of logs through the inlet to Midland's mill. Iron rings still remain in the rock along the shore where they once held the booms firmly against the rough water. The lumber business eventually vanished from the area and now a fishing lodge operates on the grave site of Collins Inlet, a mill town that was once home to 200 people. All the buildings have been either burned to the ground or swallowed up by the bush; docks for the wooden schooners and steel-hulled steam-ships have rotted along the banks; and the ring of the axe and the screech of the saw have long been silent.

This is a perfect weekend trip. You can choose any of the campsites along the way, so long as they are not already in use. Since this area is classified as Crown land, no permits are required and sites cannot be reserved. Camping is based on a first come first served basis so head out early.

The return trip is via the same route to Tyson.

Mahzenazing River in late fall.

A 3,160-metre portage makes its way between these two rolling hills to the Lake of Threenarrows.

ROUTE #4
George, Freeland, Killarney, Threenarrows, Baie Fine,
Artist, Muriel, O.S.A., Killarney, Freeland, George
Duration: 4 to 5 days

This route is for the true adventurer. Experience in canoe-tripping and a clean bill of health are essential before heading out on such a strenuous loop. In my younger days a friend and I embarked on this very route unprepared and suffered the consequences.

There were four of us: my regular canoe partner Rolf Erne, two friends from school, and myself. Rolf and I decided to take to the woods and rough it for our vacation, while the other two outdoorsmen decided to stay at the main campground with the rest of the crowded sardines. The reason for their decision to stay behind may have had something to do with a certain two outdoorswomen just down the way, on campsite 83.

As Rolf and I loaded our canoe with necessary supplies, we received an amazing amount of assistance from our two friends. In fact, we were forced to leave in such a haste that neither of us had a chance to check our equipment list.

We waved goodbye to our companions as they pushed us out into the lake, wishing us good luck and a silent good riddance.

We headed off in search of Killarney's wilds, working our way across George, Freeland and Killarney lakes (described previously). The trip was a holiday in heaven — that is, until we reached the portage to hell, a 3,160-metre path working its way over an entire mountain range towards Lake of Threenarrows.

The first incline was exhausting. The slippery rocks made our leg muscles strain to gain purchase on every foothold. The weight of the packs and canoe was finally relieved as we started heading down the slope. But the valley below was a bug-infested swamp. Our knuckles turned white as we gripped the sides of the canoe firmly, unable to swat the mosquitoes that were sucking the blood from the bulging veins of our wrists.

Just as we were about to give up hope, I saw what every portager dreams of when working towards the trail's end. Down the steep slope, through the thick forest, I could see blue peeking from behind the green foliage. We had finally found the small lake just before Threenarrows, more beautiful than I had ever imagined.

Exhausted from the long day, we soon located the closest available campsite, pitched the tent, emptied the canoe, and searched our packs for our food rations. To our horror, we discovered that the only food our friends had packed for us was a bottle of Crisco oil, a water jug filled with sugar, and a beat-up package of dried prunes. Our "good" friends had hastily dispatched us into the wilderness so they could return to greet the two female campers, and now we were left to live off the land.

With a stomach full of dried prunes and a spoon of sugar each, Rolf and I paddled out into the darkness in search of pickings from Mother Nature's larder — pike, pickerel, perch, bass, lake trout, even a meaty sunfish or lurking rock bass would do. Armed with rod and reel we drifted slowly into a protected bay.

"Boy, I hope there's a trophy-size pike just waiting to be caught tonight," I said.

My partner, who had already been affected by the sweetened prunes dipped in Crisco oil, replied with a whisper of despair, "Well, I sure hope it's not too big, because we seem to have forgotten the net."

Moments later, my rod suddenly went taut. I quickly retrieved a monster pike from its aquatic home, flipped it into the canoe, and attacked it mercilessly with the blade of my paddle.

Our mouths began to salivate as we paddled back to camp dreaming of gourmet recipes for our prize pike. The dreams turned to nightmares, however, when we realized that we had left our frying pan back with the two Casanovas.

The next day, after a breakfast of prunes and blueberries, we were forced to shorten our trip and head back to George Lake. But as our weary bodies paddled toward the sandy beach of the main campground, we witnessed something that made the ordeal we had suffered seem like a day at the circus. On one side of the beach, the two girls we had met before leaving on our adventure were busy playing frisbee with two husky weightlifter types. On the other side, our two friends, who had so eagerly cast us off unprepared, sat alone with their heads hung low.

It was a moment I'll never forget. It's one thing to chance starving to death in the interior of a provincial park but it's something else entirely to be rejected by the only eligible girls in the main camp.

If you have perfectly planned out this route, the third day should be spent touring this pocket of wilderness where three small lakes were joined by the construction of a dam on the southwestern inlet to develop the Lake of Threenarrows.

This lake, surrounded by a rugged mountain range, is quite isolated, and it is rumoured that Al Capone vacationed in the area, at a small cabin owned by an ex-mayor of Chicago.

It is said that a change is as good as a rest, so instead of repeating the extensive portage to Killarney Lake, try your luck on The Pig, a 1,530-metre old tote road that was used by loggers from 1908 to 1927. The length of this portage may be less than that of the former one, but that does not mean it is any easier. The Pig just happens to be the steepest portage in the park's interior.

Bud Hilson owns the ancient jeep you'll come across on the portage. He has a cabin on Threenarrows and since his boyhood has acted as caretaker for cabin owners on the lake, maintaining the cottages during the off-season and picking up and delivering people with his faithful four-wheeler. A large number of the cabins on the islands and shores of Killarney's interior lakes will soon be empty, for starting in May 1990 all land-use permits will no longer be renewed.

Some camps are situated on private land, such as Yoko Island, and will remain in the park.

To shorten your stay at Threenarrows, the third night can be spent on the north shore of Baie Fine, a historic anchorage for elaborate yachts and small sailing vessels. Make sure, however, that all water, especially that from The Pool, is boiled for at least five minutes before drinking. With all the boats dumping their waste before leaving the bay, the popular anchor site's name should be changed to the "Toilet Bowl."

To complete your journey, return by way of Artist, through the weeds of Muriel, and then via the familiar O.S.A. — Killarney—Freeland—George Lake route.

ROUTE #5
Bell
Duration: 2 to 3 days

An excellent weekend vacation in Killarney's interior can be had on Bell Lake. One can either paddle out from the convenient access point and choose one of the maintained sites on the lake or book a leisurely holiday at Blue Mountain Lodge, located on an island directly across from the Bell Lake access point.

The white rock of La Cloche can only be seen in the distance. Bell Lake is surrounded by a mixture of pink and black granite and the old outcrop of quartzite. The vegetation consists of mixed deciduous and conifer forest, with weathered pines standing alone on rocky islands covered in blueberries and patches of bunchberries.

If you decide to "rough it" at one of the choice campsites on Bell (named after surveyor Robert Bell, who mapped a portion of the La Cloche Mountain Range in the late 1800s), plan a day-hike up Silver Peak, the highest point of rock in this ancient range.

You can reach the old logging road leading to the main trail up to the summit by canoeing to the west end of Bell. Silver Peak was so named for the silver glare fish-

White pine exposed to the elements on top of Silver Peak, the highest point of elevation in La Cloche.

Mature bald eagle.

Blue Mountain Lodge, located within the park on Bell Lake.

ermen would see from Georgian Bay. It was once used as a home base for the Lands and Forests fire tower. Wreckage from the old tower and unsightly graffiti deface this natural landmark.

The hike takes approximately four to six hours in total and is worth every bead of sweat and tired muscle.

Many adventurers have hiked up the steep grade to Silver Peak, but one particular group turned their journey into a historical farce.

In July 1863 the steamer *Plough Boy* docked in Killarney. Aboard was a party of eight men headed by James Mc-Cormick of Toronto. The group unloaded their supplies, including several horses, wagons, buggies, dogs, hand sleds, toboggans, harnesses for both horse and dog, and a good supply of "medicinal" whiskey. Camp was made by the main street, and the men set about preparing for their expedition — not to La Cloche, but rather to the North Pole. In a month's time the farthest the men had got was to the top of Silver Peak, for they frequently returned to base camp for more "medicinal supplies." When the liquor ran out, so did the dreams of reaching the North Pole. The expedition was soon forgotten, all the equipment sold, and the party members returned home.

A short scenic canoe loop which can be completed in a single day from your campsite on Bell is another excellent way to spend your weekend in Killarney Provincial Park.

Paddling east, you make your way through a narrow channel (called Three Mile Lake) to a short lift-over. At one time a small marine railway made this section easier to portage, but paddlers took advantage of its service without bothering to keep up its general maintenance, and the owners of Blue Mountain Lodge were eventually forced to dismantle it.

Balsam Lake has one of the largest bass and pike populations in the park, so bring your tackle and you may be rewarded with a delectable shoreline lunch. While making your way through the murky green water of Balsam, be on the lookout for "Old Baldy," a resident mature bald eagle.

The raptor and I first met on Balsam while I was attempting to catch dinner in a weedy bay (without success). Showing up my angling abilities, the eagle swooped down directly behind me, plunged his powerful talons into the water and flew off grasping a two-kilogram bass.

To complete your loop, portage into Little Bell Lake, down into Chain Lake, and over a series of beaver dams. A short portage — not marked on the park map — exits into the small bay on Bell's north shore. To the east of the portage is one of my favourite campsites. On calm evenings one can often sight a family of loons at the mouth of the small creek to the left of the portage. The sound of their calling into the night stirs a deep feeling of peace and contentment.

ROUTE #6
Charlton, Frood, Cranberry, Grace, Carmichael (Nellie), Murray, Howry Creek, Charlton
Duration: 3 days

For this route, drive to Willisville and use the access point on Charlton Lake. This isolated northern entrance to Killarney Provincial Park is a gateway to the land which members of the Group of Seven believed to be a painter's paradise.

Even arriving late in the day you should still be able to make it to Grace Lake by way of Frood and Cranberry lakes. The wind from the bay usually speeds your vessel down the narrow waterway. The shallow channel joining Frood and Cranberry is littered with the rubble remains of a dam built by Group of Seven member Frank Carmichael. Carmichael built a cottage to the east. With the dam at Whitefish constantly leaking, he was forced to raise the water level in Cranberry Lake in order to navigate through to his sketching sites. To the south Carmichael made sketches for "Bay of Islands" and to the north, "Twisted Pine."

The 1,530-metre portage into Grace is the least treacherous one on the route, making its way alongside a secluded stream. There are two campsites on Grace, the farthest being more suitable for larger groups and the closest in proximity to the portage. This site was a favourite of Carmichael's. From here he would head up the ridge to the north or up the 360-metre elevation to the south, where he captured the view of the rugged landscape between Grace and Nellie lakes.

Indians from Manitoulin Island once used the exposed ridge tops as sites for their vision quests. These were occasions to discover individual identity, to build courage, and after fasting in solitude a vision would grant each brave his guardian angel.

I have always travelled in to Grace Lake solo. When you are alone in the wilds of Killarney, animals seem to wander out from hiding and you become part of their daily lives instead of just an outside observer. The little night noises lull you to sleep instead of keeping you awake. After one extensive solo adventure through the park's interior, I ended my trip by camping the last night on Grace Lake. That evening I wrote a special note in my journal: "I do not feel alone tonight, for I have the wilderness."

The second day of the route is a day of hard work and plenty of sweat. The 1,890-metre portage into Carmichael Lake, the western bay of Nellie Lake, is long and treacherous, but once you have reached beautiful Nellie you can enjoy brunch on the shores of the clearest lake in the park.

A.Y. Jackson noted this section of water in his autobiography: "Swanson proposed we should go to Nellie Lake the next day. It was some miles away, nestled in high hills. There [were] a couple of portages on the way, and at the first Swanson, a giant of a man with a small head and sharp eyes, picked up a canoe and stuck it on his head as though he were putting on a hat. There was a scow on Nellie Lake in which we embarked instead of our canoes. Two of the professors each took an oar and laboriously started rowing down the lake which was long and narrow, enclosed by big hills. After a while Swanson said, 'Give me the oars,' and he sent the scow along like a racing shell, calling our attention to the scenery as we went along."

Jackson did sketches for his famous painting "Nellie Lake" from the top of the 340-metre elevation east of the portage into Murray. The body of water he actually captured on canvas was the small bay that was later named Carmichael Lake, after his sketching companion Frank Carmichael. The saddle portage to the west (the preceding portage) was also captured by Jackson's brush, immortalizing La Cloche's rolling mounds of rock.

The portage into Murray along Notch Creek is not as rough as it is going the opposite direction. At Murray Lake the mountains seem to disappear and the hemlock and pine which surrounded Grace and Nellie change to lowland deciduous bush of maple and birch. This marks the northern section of the park, where the glorious vistas of La Cloche give way to weedy fish-filled waters.

I once spent an entire day relaxing from previous portages at my campsite east of the waterfalls. Here I enjoyed one of the best forms of entertainment staged in the northern woods: I simply watched the crazy antics of everyday camp critters.

First there was a chipmunk who persistently skittered around camp in search of peanuts, raisins and other dropped or discarded camp food. Then there was a red squirrel who kept my attention throughout the day by clipping cones from an old pine tree. The squirrel worked to no avail, however, as the tree branches hung over the water's edge and the clipped cones plunged into the lake. Later a song sparrow danced around camp, at one point sprinting across my dinner plate, leaving prints in my evening stew.

The third and final day takes you along Howry Creek, where raccoons wander through the entanglement of alder and poplar, where herons flush from floating bog mats, where otter families dip under your canoe and goshawks soar above the creek bed. Along the banks of this murky waterway are scattered remnants of the La Cloche gold-mining era (which ended in the late 1950s). Rotten boats, timber, rusted barbed wire, the remains of mine shafts, and even a squatter's farm have been abandoned along the slow-moving creek.

Take your time paddling down the gentle current, for this section of the route is alive with a diversity of flora and fauna. Hummingbirds hum around the dark-red cardinal flowers, warblers and wrens bounce across the shrubs which decorate the banks, and bears sniff out grubs among the rotten debris left by miners and loggers. (Just below the 230-metre portage, a black bear actually made away with a tube of toothpaste from my pack while I was busy carrying my canoe down the path. So if you're in the area, be on the lookout for a bear with a gleaming smile.)

The creek finally winds its way out to Charlton Lake, where the winds that helped you down Frood Lake now battle against you. A few islands dot the lake, and these provide welcome spots to rest aching shoulders and bandage blistered palms.

Eventually the unpleasant moment comes when you round the bend to the left and sight your vehicle parked at the docking site in Willisville, signalling the end of your trip into the heart of the La Cloche Mountain Range.

ROUTE #7

George, Freeland, Kakakise, Carlyle, Johnnie, Crooked, Brush Camp, Bell, David, Great Mountain, Fish, Gem, Howry, Murray, Nellie, Grace, Cranberry Bay, Frood, Whitefish Falls, Storehouse Bay, Iroquois Bay, North Channel, McGregor Bay, Baie Fine, Artist Creek, Muriel, O.S.A., Killarney, Freeland, George
Duration: 8 to 10 days

This is obviously one of the longest possible routes in the park, covering almost the entire area by canoe. If you wish to shorten it, a good idea is to make plans to park a second vehicle by Charlton Lake access point to the north, cutting the La Cloche loop in half.

If arriving in the afternoon I try and plan it so as to paddle and portage through George, Freeland and Kakakise lakes (previously mentioned) and camp at Carlyle Lake the first night out. The site between Carlyle and Terry lakes has always been my favourite choice. In fact I've always looked forward to waking early the second day and paddling across Terry to catch a breakfast of perch from below the small waterfalls.

After a hearty breakfast, try to traverse Carlyle and Johnnie lakes before the mid-morning breeze develops into a dreadful gale. Without warning, the wind can come up and it can stop a canoe as effectively as a brick wall. Everything else can be perfect — the sky unspoiled by clouds, the sun burning down — but a simple build-up of breath from above can halt all progress.

Johnnie Lake, originally called Brush Camp Lake, was surveyed in 1892 by W. Galbraith, who wrote: "The country is generally broken and rocky and to the west of Brush Camp Lake high hills of grey granite rock . . . ." (Another lake on this route is now called Brush Camp Lake.) Although the quartzite mountains are visible to the north, the white rock is absent around this lake.

The route initially travels northeast, but then veers west into a large bay called Crooked Lake. On the north side of Crooked Lake is a waterfall flowing over a 30-metre ridge separating Ruth Roy and Crooked lakes.

Once through to Brush Camp Lake, cottage development disappears. To reach David Lake, where you should plan to camp the third night, choose between the portage in and out of Clearsilver Lake or follow a series of small portages connecting Log Boom Lake, Bell Lake and David Creek. I much prefer the latter route, especially in the spring, when the 720-metre portage to David Creek can be omitted due to high water levels.

Campsites situated along David's western shore present excellent views of the sun setting behind the northern

Murray Lake,
located inside the
park's northern
boundary.

Notch Creek Valley, between Murray and Nellie lakes.

ridges and of refreshing sunrises burning up the morning mist along the shore.

Make sure you start off early the next day. You want to complete the 2,540-metre portage, beginning at the northwest end of David and continuing on to Great Mountain Lake, well before the mosquitoes begin to warm their wings in the mid-morning rays. The pockets of mud and water to the west of the portage are known breeding grounds for thousands of these vampires of the forest.

Great Mountain Lake is an excellent place to stop for brunch. This isolated spot, where the well-known bush pilot Rusty Blakey had an old aluminum cabin, offers a breathtaking view of sheer, shimmering quartzite. Though bald and golden eagles are often spotted soaring above the cliffs, many are mistaken for turkey vultures. This scavenger, identified by its V-shaped wing pattern, is ideally suited to this open landscape. A relatively new species to Killarney, the turkey vulture mops up leftovers too rotten for consumption by other predators.

When exiting Great Mountain Lake, take the 470-metre portage as opposed to the trickle of water connecting Great Mountain with Fish Lake. Old flumes, axe heads and crosscut saws have been found in this creek, indicating the location of one of Killarney's early timber-cutting camps.

From Fish Lake on, feel free to cast a line for pike or bass, which populate the majority of lakes along the northern section of the park.

Before heading west to Murray Lake, make sure that you have checked with park staff concerning water levels. If it is a dry season, it may be best to travel north by way of Round Otter, Rocky, Crow, Van Winkle and Cat lakes to avoid the painstaking task of poling through the black ooze of decaying plant matter (commonly referred to as "loon scat").

When water levels are high, Gem Lake and Howry Lake are full of fish, so choose to travel this route if you can. Your efforts will be rewarded with a fresh fish-fry for your evening meal.

The portage from Howry into Murray has been extended to almost the complete length of Howry Creek. Murray Lake is weedy, but it's best to camp here rather than attempt the rugged portage into Nellie before dark. Two sites are available on the lake, both are on high ground, and if it wasn't for the thick growth of aquatic vegetation strangling the shore, the camps would be perfect.

The fourth day is one of the most exhausting of the trip, so make an early start and prepare for the worst. You finally leave the brush and muskeg of the park's northern landscape and once again enter the La Cloche Mountain Range.

The portage into Nellie's western bay (Carmichael Lake) begins in the centre of Murray Lake, where Notch Creek can be heard falling down the steep quartzite cliff. The path's initial 90 metres leads up a steep incline to the left of the waterfall, but once you reach the first ridge, the portage levels off and winds around a swamp on the upland plateau. After the portage crosses Notch Creek, which flows into the swamp, it makes its way up the side of a treacherous gorge.

Nellie Lake has to be one of the prettiest lakes in Killarney, situated almost 23 metres higher in elevation than its neighbouring lakes. It is also the clearest body of water in the park, with 28-metre visibility.

The portage to Grace Lake (1,890 metres) is just as rugged as the path to Carmichael. I'll never forget one fall morning when, while making my way to Carmichael from Grace in the midst of a violent hail storm, I was suddenly re-routed after a large yellow birch came crashing down across the trail right in front of me.

When you reach Grace, choose a campsite, then either paddle the lake's perimeter, swim out to one of the picturesque islands, or explore the high ridges surrounding the lake, where such famous painters as Frank Carmichael and Robert Bateman have sketched Killarney's northern beauty.

This paradise was once transformed into a private hell for me when a storm forced me to hole up in my flimsy nylon dwelling for two entire days. The tent rose and flapped and shuddered, pinned down by my weight alone. I waited for the inevitable disaster, when poles would snap, material would rip and my limp body would be tossed to and fro across the open landscape.

On day five treat yourself to an injection of civilization by portaging out of Grace for 1,530 metres along a small stream and into Cranberry Bay, Frood Lake and finally Whitefish Falls, where you can purchase a can of cold pop from the general store. Make sure to satisfy all your addictions at Whitefish before heading on, because the next two days are devoted to constant paddling through Storehouse Bay, Iroquois Bay and along the North Channel, where voyageurs once travelled on their way to Fort La Cloche.

The insignificant islands, small bays and rock bluffs, crowned with a few scrubby jack pine, grass, shrubs and lichens, seem countless while making your way through this confusion of rock and water. At times only the sound of the raven cracking its throat can be heard.

Before navigating through this western section of La Cloche, check with park staff for definite directions. There is an access point to Iroquois Bay from the fourth inlet south of the marinas. A channel, known locally as Muskeg Channel, works its way to a short portage into Iroquois Bay.

After passing three islands positioned in a straight row, the route angles south between Iroquois Island and the mainland. It then changes its direction abruptly towards the North Channel, where steep quartzite outcrops pierce the cool waters.

The landscape appears even more lonely upon entering the East Channel, where a few good campsites are available for the night.

The paddle from McGregor Bay to Baie Fine can be a hard one, especially travelling solo against a steady wind. I once chose to paddle the length of Baie Fine on a calm moonlit night, rather than battle the wind and waves during the day. That was an unforgettable evening. The night was filled with sights and sounds. Around midnight I stopped paddling and coasted along the shoreline. My sixth sense suddenly caused me to turn around and I came eye to eye with a timber wolf. The wolf stared at me and a spell was cast in this dark wilderness. My mind quickly filled with fear of the unknown. I considered halting my extended solo trip into Killarney right then and there. I found myself questioning my sanity and my safety — alone in La Cloche, surrounded by unknown territory, not another human for miles. I thrust my wooden blade into the water and hastily made my escape. A few minutes later, the light of the moon illuminated the dark figure of a lone wolf standing on a rocky ledge. The wolf was following me along the shore. Powered by an inner magnet and embarrassed by my previous cowardly actions, I did the unthinkable. I paddled toward shore. Without warning, the wolf howled into the night air. I was inexplicably moved by the wolf's cry and spent the rest of the night drifting through the "lonely land" never once feeling alone.

In addition to wolves, coyotes, otters, herons and beavers inhabit the heavy weeds of Artist Creek as it nears Muriel Lake. You should reach this area by day seven, with enough spare time to climb the ridges to the north of O.S.A. Lake and view your accomplishment through the "Bay of Isles."

Always add an extra day or two in case rainstorms or heavy winds slow you down. From O.S.A. it should take only a few hours to canoe to George Lake by way of Killarney and Freeland lakes, so enjoy a hearty breakfast before ending your extended La Cloche loop adventure.

Frood Lake. Frank Carmichael once constructed a dam here so he could paddle further along Cranberry Bay to his favourite sketching sites.

Many choose to navigate the North Channel by kayak rather than open canoe.

Additional Information

LODGES IN THE KILLARNEY AREA:

Blue Mountain Lodge
   P.O. Box 66, Station B
   Sudbury, Ontario
   (705) 287-2197

Located on Bell Lake, in the northeast corner of the park, Blue Mountain is the perfect family resort, featuring private log cottages and fine home-cooked meals served in the dining room. A super place for the canoeist, hiker, fisherman, or outdoor enthusiast. They also rent canoes.

Killarney Mountain Lodge
   (705) 287-2242
   1-800-461-1117

The Sportsman's Inn
   (705) 287-2411

Killarney Mountain Lodge and the Sportsman's Inn offer fine dining and comfortable accommodations in the town of Killarney. Perfect for yacht owners sailing the bay.

Killarney Outfitters
   (705) 287-2828
   Killarney Outfitters are located five minutes west of the provincial park. This is a good place to rent canoes and camping equipment.

Charlton Lake Lodge and Bear Skin Lodge
   Hunting and fishing camps located across from the northern access point at Willisville. Canoes can be rented from both camps, and a laundromat, small store and showers are available at Charlton Lake Lodge. Contact Killarney Provincial Park for reservation information.

Rouche "Roche" Campground
   Located in the town of Killarney, along the southeast shore of Killarney Bay, this is an excellent place for the camper with a large boat and motor (which the provincial park bans).

CHURCHES
   St. Bonaventure Church is a Roman Catholic church welcoming all denominations. Services are held Thursday to Saturday at 7 p.m. and Sunday at 9:30 a.m.

LAUNDRY FACILITIES
   Sportsman's Inn Hotel and Baie du Fois Restaurant

SOUVENIR SHOPS
Quarterdeck:
   9 a.m. to 12 p.m. — 1 p.m. to 5 p.m.

Rockhouse Inn:
   (breakfast and lunch) 7 a.m. to 5 p.m.
   (gift shop) 7 a.m. to 9 p.m.

Pitfield's General Store:
   8 a.m. to 10 p.m. Mon-Sun

Bay du Fois Restaurant:
   8 a.m. to 9 p.m. Mon-Sun
   Canoe rentals, supplies, gas bar, restaurant with excellent
blueberry pie

M.S. *Chi-Cheemaun* (reservations)
   1-800-265-3163

HEALTH CENTRE
   Nursing Staff: 287-2300

AMBULANCE:
   287-2521

POLICE:
   Killarney has a five-person OPP detachment
   287-2881

KILLARNEY PROVINCIAL PARK:
   Killarney Provincial Park
   Killarney, Ontario
   P0M 2A0
   Information (705) 287-2900
   Reservations (705) 287-2800

Bibliography

Father Couture. "Manitoulin (1600-1800) Its First Inhabitants – Its First Missionaries," *The Recorder,* 1912.

Father Couture. "History of Manitoulin Island 1600-1800," *Katonik Anishinabe Enakamigak* (Catholic Indian News).

Darroch, Lois. *Bright Land: A Warm Look at Arthur Lismer.* Toronto: Merritt Publishing Co. Ltd., 1981.

Debicki, R.L. *Geology and Scenery,* Killarney Provincial Park Area Ontario (Ontario Geological Survey Guidebook No. 6): with permission of E.G. Pye, Director, Ontario Geological Survey, Ministry of Natural Resources, 1982.

Drew, Wayland, and Bruce Littlejohn. *Superior: The Haunted Shore.* Gage Publishing Ltd., 1975.

Lady Dufferin. *My Canadian Journal,* 1872-1878.

The Friends of Killarney Provincial Park and the Ontario Ministry of Natural Resources. *Killarney Provincial Park Hiking Trails.* Killarney: 1989.

Groves, Naomi Jackson. *A.Y.'s Canada: Pencil Drawings by A.Y. Jackson.* Toronto: Clark, Irwin and Co., 1968.

Jackson, A.Y. *A Painter's Country: The Autobiography of A.Y. Jackson,* Centennial Edition. Toronto: Clarke, Irwin and Co., 1958, 1967.

Killarney Provincial Park Management Plan, Park Management Planning Series; Ministry of Natural Resources, 1985.

Loosemore, Adele. "Killarney Past and Present," *Mid-North Monitor,* Nov. 5, 1980; Feb. 20, 1980; Jan. 23, 1980.

McQuarrie, W. John, editor-publisher. *Through the Years,* Vols. 21, 26, 46, 60 and 69. Mid-North Printers and Publishers Ltd., 1983.

Pitfield, Bruce. "Down Memory Lane," Gore Bay *Recorder,* Sept. 14, 1983; Aug. 14, 1985; Sept. 7, 1983.

Pugh, D. "Killarney Provincial Park and Environs." Interpretation Report, 1970.

Shields, Tom. "Dream of A.J. Casson — Revisiting La Cloche."

Stacey, Robert. "Whiterock: Eric Aldwinkle's O.S.A. Lake Description and Guide" (date unknown).

Georgian Bay shoreline near the navigation light at Red Rock Point.

Sunset on O.S.A. Lake.
"Wilderness is the raw material out of which man has hammered the artifact called civilization."

Aldo Leopold (1949)